A SKELETON CREW ANTHOLOGY

Folklore, Fated Mates, and Deleted Scenes

DAHLIA DONOVAN

HOT TREE PUBLISHING

For information, contact the publisher, Hot Tree Publishing.

WWW.HOTTREEPUBLISHING.COM

Editing: Hot Tree Editing

Cover Designer: BookSmith Design

Map Design: The Illustrated Page Book Design

E-book ISBN: 978-1-923252-48-6

Paperback ISBN: 978-1-923252-49-3

For James.

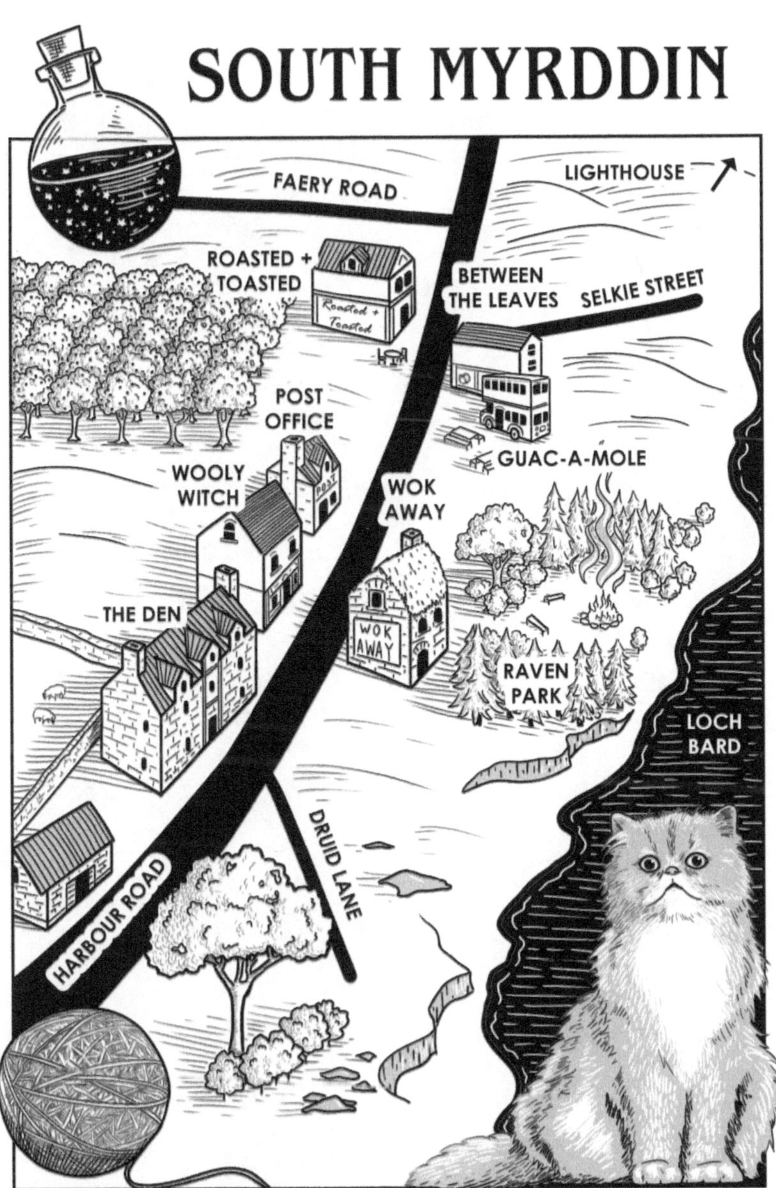
SOUTH MYRDDIN
FAERY ROAD
LIGHTHOUSE
ROASTED + TOASTED
Roasted + Toasted
BETWEEN THE LEAVES
SELKIE STREET
POST OFFICE
POST
GUAC-A-MOLE
WOOLY WITCH
WOK AWAY
WOK AWAY
THE DEN
RAVEN PARK
LOCH BARD
HARBOUR ROAD
DRUID LANE

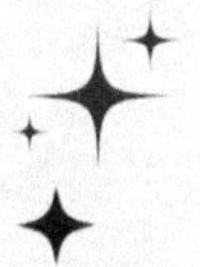

HER NAME WAS NESS

Learn the truth behind the myth of Loch Ness. Follow the dramatic tale of Ness MacDougal and the two who hold her heart. Beset on all sides by warring warlocks, druids, and vampires. Can the three lovers find their escape before her family castle is brought down around them?

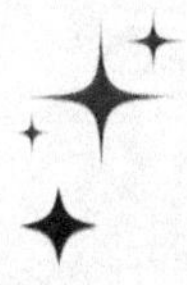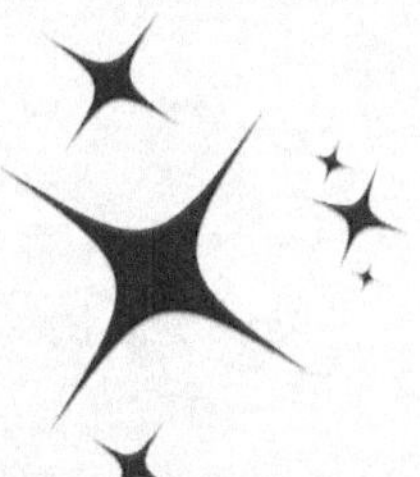

JANUARY 17, 2024

Bram,

Here's the translation of that eighteenth-century book. It's not Ness MacDougal's poetry like you thought. Well, it does include some of her poetry. It's the journal of one of her lovers.

A fae or half-fae rumoured to be the origin of the Baobhan Sith in Scottish folklore. I remember reading about a Morag who seduced a powerful witch and warlock, stealing their lives away.

I'm sure you know more about her than I would since you're mentioned—as is Emrys. Why didn't you say you knew Ness?

The journal was written in a coded form of fourteenth-century Gaelic. Something she developed herself. Translating it was a nightmare.

but I've managed to put some of the entries into modern English, though not all of them. Some were too damaged to decipher.

I did my best. You owe me snacks. Many snacks. I had a migraine by the time I got the first page translated.

Hyde

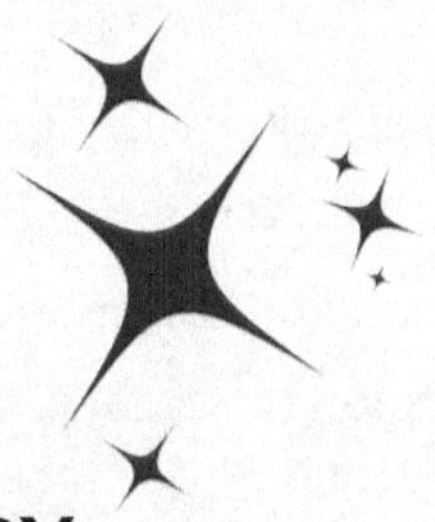

JOURNAL ENTRY

MARCH 1880

Their hearts doth meld with mine,
Love lost, then found.
Our hearts are intertwined.
No being can change our fate.
~Ness MacDougal

Of four things, I can always be certain. Her name is Ness MacDougal, her hair is still as fiery as her temper, her eyes are as brilliant green as the scales on her serpent form, and we love her as we did then. It has never wavered.

We love her—and she adores us in return.

Her name is Nessie. She gives her heart so freely that I have no compunctions at realigning worlds for her. A hundred years later, I find myself with no

regrets. I imagine even a millennium would fail to change my mind.

The following journal is a mostly true telling of our tale. If you have managed to understand the words within—congratulations. I am kind to friend and foe. And yet, still, there is nothing I would change.

Perhaps it is less of a tale and more of a collection of my meandering thoughts. The world we left has changed for the better, it seems. Yet we cannot return to it. We will not.

This is my second venture back to this realm. I have laid flowers where we once danced under a starry sky. It is a melancholy place now. All remembered joy is but a fleeting wisp of a memory.

The loch feels haunted and the castle broken, crumbling walls and overgrown gardens. It is no longer the home that it once was. An ancient relic of what seems a distant dream faded into nothing.

I am Morag. Fae. Wielder of wild magic. She of the Unseelie Court. My hair is wild and dark as a raven's feathers. My eyes are a stormy blue like the loch after a storm.

Ness is rumoured to be half-fae. All sorceress. Poet. Witch. Temptress. Glorious divine being. Her untamed red curls and her startling green eyes are unmatched. She is a goddess in mortal form.

For half a century, we revelled together until change

blew in on a foul winter wind. It is a glorious time. We never even know a part of our hearts is missing until a pounding comes to the castle gates.

Our third is a warlock—Codrin. He is strong and powerful. The tattoos on his skin have faded with time, but he remains the third pillar of our relationship.

He joins us as the one shining light in the darkest of times. The great philosophers all warn of how things must change. None ever fully speak of how painful and difficult it can be.

We come through it alive but not unscathed. Marks will live on in our psyche forever. Still, we have found some measure of comfort amongst ourselves.

It all starts with the great storm of 1760. A winter gale like every other before it. Yet it brings the beginning of the end of one chapter and the start of our greatest adventure.

JOURNAL ENTRY
FEBRUARY 1760

The wind howled.
Ice and snow fell.
On horse, he came,
A wildfire on a winter's gale.
~Ness MacDougal

Today is bitterly cold. Castle MacDougal sits on the loch of the same name, keeping out enemies but not so much winter's icy blast. Fires roar in every hearth in a fruitless attempt to combat the powerful gale.

The MacDougals have built their small fortress on the north corner of the inlet. The strong family of witches, warlocks, and shifters has been content to seclude themselves in the wilds of Scotland, though only one remains. When Ness's mother fell in love with

a fae of the Unseelie Court, they vanished when the poor lass was barely eighteen. She manages alone now.

Or so the story goes. There is no proof of the fae part of her family. I believe it to be true, but who can tell? With their absence went any chance to know for certain.

Ness is a power serpent shifter who wields healing magic in a way more akin to fae than witch. She is kind and gentle despite her temper. A person who is not meant for solitary life despite our first meeting.

Years later, I found her alone, managing the castle with only a local shifter and a druid checking in on her occasionally. As a member of the court, I took it upon myself to help her. Love had never been a part of the plan.

Alas, the cold is making me melancholy for the past few days. I intend to commit the day's events to this journal, starting with a visitor who found his way to us through the wind and snow.

Codrin cel Mare.

Codrin the Great.

He of the principality of Moldavia.

His black hair has flakes of snow glittering brightly in the flickering candlelight. A warlock on a diplomatic mission from the council of warlocks. His black eyes glint with power and mischief.

I know we are in trouble.

Ness.

Dear Ness.

Her heart has never met a stranger. She welcomes him with open arms, sending his weary horse to the stables to warm up and be cared for. Our attention remains on the enigmatic warlock who drips snow onto the stone floor.

Ness peels off his outer cloak, setting it by the largest hearth to dry. We strip him out of his clothes. He is soaked to the bone by the time we drag him out of the cold.

His body is covered with black ink tattoos. I recognise some as marks of his status amongst the warlocks. Others have to be connected to his family. The crest I know to be from an exiled royal line, one that still has those who want them dead.

No matter how I caution Ness that he is not one of her stray serpents to nurse back to health, I can see the desire in her eyes. And for truth, in my heart, I feel the same. Something about Codrin cel Mare is drawing us in. I know not whether it will be for good or ill.

The die is cast when we raise the castle gates.

Exhaustion settles into our visitor quickly. He does not provide much beyond his initial introduction. We barely get broth mixed with healing herbs into him before he falls into a deep sleep.

We sit by his bedside late into the night—Ness insists. He may need a tincture or poultice.

Despite my best efforts, Ness has already become intrigued and attached to the man of mystery. There is no arguing with her. I have learned that lesson well over decades.

After a while, I send Ness off to rest. She never does well without sufficient sleep. On the other hand, I can go days without suffering any ill effects. Her temper is not a monster I want to test in the midst of a winter gale.

With the first watch mine, I sit by his bedside, listening to the wind howling, the crackling fire, and his slightly laboured breathing while I write the days' happenings. His clothes have been taken to clean and dry. What will his sudden appearance in our quiet life bring?

A fell omen?

A signal of change?

I hesitate to draw on the ether to peek into the future. The cards are not always right, and neither are runes. Nothing is ever fully set in stone. And I have found the search for things to come often leads to trouble.

We have opened the door to something new. I hope we do not live to regret it.

My heart tells me that we will not. My mind is as ever the more cynical of the two. Change, whether good or bad, is always a cease of upheaval.

None of us can say what the end of this story will bring.

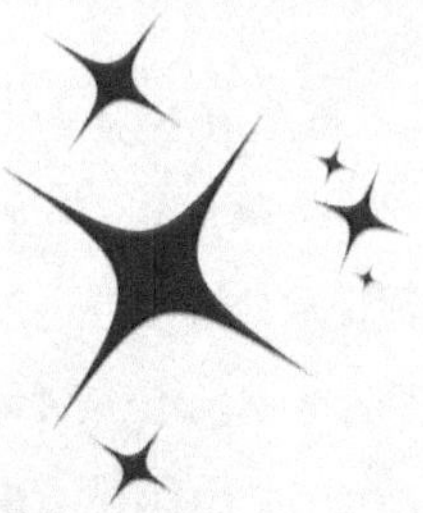

JOURNAL ENTRY

JUNE 1760

The moon hath risen and fallen.
It never lingers.
Three hearts hath met in darkness,
With a love unbidden.
~Ness MacDougal

Time passes swiftly. Four months have gone in the blink of an eye. My pen has been still for too long, so I pick it up once again. I never intend to neglect this journal, personal though it may be. I also never want another to read my often rambling thoughts.

I have always found a measure of comfort in allowing words to flow from my quill. Perhaps, when I have faded to memory, the world will remember us. No matter how I try to convince her, Ness shows no interest in exploring the fae realm with me.

Maybe one day.

Codrin, despite my expectations, remains with us after the storm. It did last far longer than expected. Poor South Myrddin, west of us on the coast, fairs poorly. Much of it is destroyed. Emrys stopped at the castle on his way home to rebuild.

His parting words to Codrin instil little hope for the success of his diplomatic quest. Emrys claims the druids have no intentions of parlaying with the warlocks or vampires unless they cease their attempts at controlling the Highlands. Neither of the two men appears optimistic of that happening.

Ness sent aid to the little foundling village on the coast through Emrys—a special place that never involves itself in the turmoil going on around it. Codrin did make a promise to keep warlocks from it— an oath sworn in magic and blood.

I pity any warlock who attempts harm upon South Myrddin. Codrin changed our world drastically when he rode into it. He has failed to complete his original quest but seems content to remain with us.

Today has been quite idyllic for the most part. The sun shines with nary a cloud in the sky. Ness drags us to the loch to frolic in the waters.

Stripped of our clothes and jewels, the cool waters wash over our skin. A more beautiful sight in this realm or others, I have never seen than Ness

MacDougal in all her glory. Oftentimes, she shifts into her serpent form, slithering through the loch with an ease before popping back up with her dripping red hair flying.

Codrin's eyes, like my own, are drawn to her glistening body. Her breasts are visible above the gentle waves. Moths to her flame. If she is the goddess Aphrodite, we faithfully worship at her altar. A baptism of love and adoration under the warmth of a summer sun.

In the shadows of Castle MacDougal, we explore the lines, curves, and scars of one another's bodies. Cartographers with the sole purpose of mapping out pleasure. Fingers soothe and tease. Mouths follow.

We hunger for one another and never stop until we are sated. I have never believed in soulmates. Love? Yes. Somehow, though, this feels different.

Codrin's strength and aura draw us to him. We trace the lines of his tattoos with our tongues. We find a rhythm between our bodies, riding out the pleasure together.

Soulmates.

Our lives have become hopelessly intertwined in a matter of months. Codrin has not left. Cannot. He claims his heart will not take the separation, so he remains with us.

If I but turn my mind to imagining him leaving, my

own heart begins to break. He stays. I have no idea what the future may hold for us.

Pleasure. Love. Joy.

I hope whatever conflict is brewing amidst the various factions remains outside the castle walls. We have a chance to build our own utopia together. It must last.

Sweet Ness.

Ness has no care for what might be on the horizon. She has us. I see the truth in Codrin's eyes, however. He understands the delicate balance in the Highlands may be upset if pushed by druids, warlocks, or vampires, the three largest and most powerful factions.

While a king rules on the throne, true power in the Highlands goes to the individual covens. As a ranking member of the Unseelie Court, I remain above the fracas. We can retreat to a separate realm to avoid conflict—our chosen tactic for a millennium.

But my heart. My heart remains here with a shifter and a warlock. My chosen path means difficulties lie ahead for the three of us. Will they submit to travelling through ley and mist to my beloved fae realm? Will they make the sacrifice of never being able to return? While fae may cross freely between worlds, others have only a one-way trip. I hesitate to ask the question for fear of disappointment.

It has been idyllic. Highland weather is not always

so kind. Our repast happens late in the evening, as we are reluctant to bid the day farewell.

Lingering kisses.

Soft caresses.

All the flowery words from the first flush of attraction.

The sun sets long before I find myself with pen in hand. I can still taste them on my tongue. No words will adequately express how they have made me feel.

And I have no desire to waste time with prose. The siren call of my lovers is impossible to ignore. Let the world bicker. I have pleasure to prolong.

JOURNAL ENTRY
AUGUST 1760

First berries plucked from the bush,
Crops ripen for the cutting.
My lovers dance naked by the fire,
Worshipping under a bright harvest
    moon.
~Ness MacDougal

Codrin remains with us. He shows no signs of tiring of our company. He is as hopelessly enthralled with us as we are with him.

His presence adds a layer to our Lùnastal celebrations. It is not often a warlock, witch, and fae come together for it—outside of South Myrddin, where everyone is welcome. The fields around the castle, along with its gardens, are ripe for harvest, so we offer our thanks.

The larder will be full for the coming winter months. There is much to do to prepare. Ness has a good head on her shoulders for managing it all.

The fires are still burning outside. I swear I can hear druids chanting across the moors. Lùnastal causes all of us to reflect on the seeds we have planted throughout the past months, for good or ill.

We have blessed the cattle and fields. It has been a good harvest. It will be a good harvest.

Rituals are sacred and secret. Yet we find a middle ground between us under a harvest moon. I have never joined a warlock on this day—or for any other ceremony in a hundred-plus years of existence.

The light fluidity of my own sacred space melds with the warm fire of Ness and the grounded earth of Codrin. Perfection is an impossibility, yet we have found the closest amalgamation to it within one another.

As the world around us continues to turn, we have found a quiet pocket to ourselves. I worry about the factions vying for control. They have paused for celebration and harvest, but the hounds will bray for blood once again.

Our joy, for now, remains untouched.

As I write, I watch my lovers sleep by the fire. Their naked bodies intertwine. A masterpiece no artist can ever dream of recreating.

Ness's body partially covers Codrin's. Her wild red hair fans across him, hiding his tattoos from view. I am enthralled all over again.

A single length of forest-green silk is draped across my desk. It glistens in the candlelight. We have used it to tie ourselves together.

A handfasting on Lùnastal.

A promise.

A vow.

For a year and a day.

May our love remain unchanged and unwavering. For years, I have fought to be untethered. Yet, for love and lust, I bind myself to a witch and warlock. Mortals. Beings with an end to their days.

A bouquet of honeysuckle sits on my desk and mocks my melancholic doubts. Love and devotion. The sweet scent of the petals reminds me of those promises made. Some days of the wheel are for reflection, others for grieving. This has been one of joy and abundance. Not all harvests are so blessed by the spirits.

Ness spends a portion of each day swimming in snake form. Today has been no exception. She never listens when I caution her. The villagers will think Loch MacDougal is haunted by a serpent. She only laughs.

Who is going to believe a loch is inhabited by a ghostly serpent? Her question is not entirely illogical. Yet I am not so sure. I have seen people and creatures of every variety turn superstitious and paranoid over the slightest unexplained oddity.

And who am I to judge when I join her much of the time?

On evenings such as this, it is hard to think about an end to our idyllic time. We have known much love and pleasure. Long days lost in the worship of one another's bodies. The world is unsettled.

Some of the Highland fae have returned home. Much of the unseelies and seelies have gone. Bram remains, as do I. We, as a court, have stayed out of bubbling tension in Scotland. I am unsure of whether we can continue to do so.

As the candle burns low, my thoughts are drawn more and more to the future. I am to visit the court in the coming year. I am loath to leave my lovers alone, not with how everything is brewing.

The quiet that harvest has brought will not last long. I have sent word to Bram. He stands a better chance of helping calm the situation, if only by defusing matters through confusion.

My fellow fae has a wildness that has never been tamed. He flits about the Highlands, never staying in one place for long. Like many, he seems to have developed a soft spot for the foundlings of South Myrddin.

The wild one is not known for intervening in the affairs of others unless he can cause mischief. Fae by birth and by nature. He is also too wrapped up in the magic he weaves with his music. I can only hope he is amenable to deflecting trouble.

Peace in the Highlands is vital to more than just the three of us in Castle MacDougal. Disrupting the careful balance between vampires, warlocks, and druids can have dire consequences. We have spoken with Emrys; he agrees wholeheartedly, if only because of his dear foundlings.

He is hesitant to attempt to draw the vampires into conversation. His love affair with Jonatan Pacheco is a well-disguised secret. Another bit of potential fuel for the fires beginning to burn. One, I imagine, will not end without a broken heart or two.

With the last flicker of candlelight, I will end this somewhat faithful telling of our Lùnastal celebration. What more can I commit to memory? How soft lips met beside a roaring fire? Hands touch. Bodies move. How we three wind together like vines of ivy, crawling towards the sky in search of the sun?

The spirits sup from our pleasure, love, and joy— and we have much of it to give. A blessing upon our union. Three hearts combine, forever and a day. We can weather the coming storm.

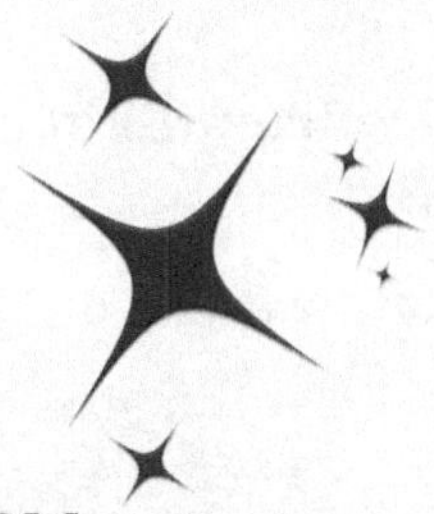

JOURNAL ENTRY

OCTOBER 1760

The chill of Samhain night approaches,
It settles deep within my bones.
Spirits stalk the moors unfettered,
They beat out a ghostly rhythm to the
     living.
~Ness MacDougal

Of all the turns of the wheel, Samhain is the one most sacred to Ness. Her heart aches for lost loved ones. She sits with her ancestors alone through the night.

As the sole living member of Clan MacDougal, she is, I think, sometimes lonely, even with Codrin and me around. The lone serpent shifter. She alone carries her family legacy.

Today, though, she communes with family.

I have stayed closer to the castle. Candles are lit, as

are the fires in all the hearths. Cauldrons bubble with fruits, herbs, and dried flowers—a blend Codrin claims is a warlock tradition for Samhain night.

Our feast is prepared for us and as an offering to the spirits. The table is laid for Ness's return. We will soothe her sadness together.

The days since Lùnastal have been fraught with tension. Codrin and Emrys have tried in vain to calm tempers between the warlocks and druids. Neither wants the actions of one rogue warlock to ruin the peace of the Highlands.

It has come down to that. One lone warlock who has chosen death and destruction. Codrin fears he will lead the coven as a whole onto a path from which none can return.

There are so few rules in this world when it comes to ritual and practice. This work seems intent on breaking all of them. He cares not for the droves of witches, druids, or any other person or creature.

The discontent begins small, yet he has fanned those flames continually. I only hope the world does not burn along with his desire. So many are content to live peacefully, and I refuse to believe one warlock will be allowed to ruin it all, but men have done far more foolish things in this world.

It is late. I once again write by candlelight. A full

moon is overhead—an auspicious addition to our Samhain night.

In a small wooded copse outside the castle walls to the south of the loch, the remnants of our small feast remain on the altar. Our offering to the spirits, the goddess, fae, god, whatever beings are in the ether listening and watching.

Our stomachs are pleasantly full. We have supped of our feast and one another. Our pleasure and worship of one another is another offering of sorts.

The bonfire has slowly died out; I can see the last of the embers from the window. By morning, nothing will remain of it or the feast.

There is a heaviness within me. A worry for the future. No matter how I try to push those thoughts away, I cannot help my fears for the coming months.

Whatever upheaval is on the horizon, it may affect all of us. It is not going to be pleasant. I hope we can withstand the storm.

I fear my pen has grown repetitious. My thoughts circle like a whirling dervish. I do not know how the next months will transform our precious Highlands.

Soon, I will join my beloveds in bed. I shall throw myself at their mercy. Allow myself to be cocooned in their embrace. If nothing else, it is a far better use of my time than ruminating over impending troubles again and again.

Before I close the grimoire and my eyes for the night, I shall better commit to memory our evening in further detail. I am nigh on immortal. Days easily blend together and become forgotten, but there are special ones I hope to remember.

In the small grove, our feast lay on a table specifically made for this purpose, beside the altar I helped to build. A blanket of jewel-coloured leaves covered the trees above and the ground below. A flock of ravens sat on various branches, joining us for the celebration. Some might consider them a fell omen, but they are feathered friends of Codrin's, and they came to add their cries to our revelry.

It was otherworldly.

Our feast was one of plenty. We carefully preserved all the remnants of our glorious harvest for the coming winter months. A portion of roasted pheasant and fallow deer joined both our table and the altar—a gift to the land, the spirits, and all who came to sup with us.

We took turns braiding our hair with dried flowers. First, Ness's wild red locks were tamed with a message of love and hope. My black hair was threaded with a floral note for courage and wisdom. Codrin's thick brown hair contained ones connected to an ancient warlock rite—one he refused to share despite our attempts at persuasion.

For all its joy and pleasure, a sombre note found its way through our night of feasting. Ness picked up the song, and we joined in. A dirge for all we have lost in the past and all we might do in the future.

It was how we chose to end the evening.

Naked in mind, body, and song.

The ravens still caw outside. I can hear their cries on the wind. Codrin claims they are friends… messengers.

In the flickering candlelight, it is hard not to sense a foreboding tone to their message. If nothing else, they certainly seem to be warning of us. I am unclear what or why. They have never been quite so vocal, even with Codrin in the castle. They sense change as much as I do.

In two short months, the new year is upon us. Codrin plans to approach Emrys once again. He does not want to simply surrender to some inevitable conflict.

None of us do.

None of us wish to see three warring covens.

For all of our innate strength and power, we cannot bend others to our will. It is that which the one faction of warlocks wishes to do. I do not blame Codrin for wanting to make another attempt.

I am simply afraid it will not go the way he wishes.

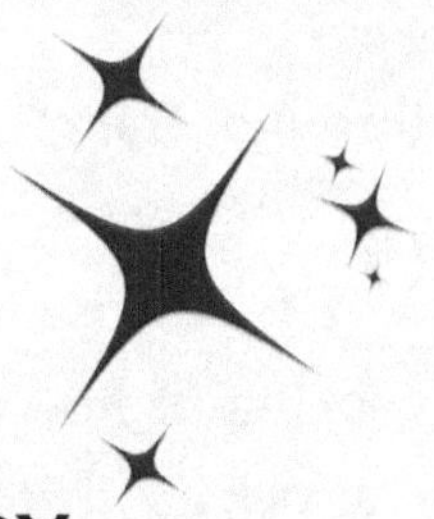

JOURNAL ENTRY
JANUARY 1761

Oh, icy fingers,
doth grip my heart.
Oh, dearest loves,
must we part?
~Ness MacDougal

An icy fog settles over the loch. It drifts down from the moors to cover us. A damp, chilled blanket that smothers the lingering joy from midwinter.

Ness smells snow in the air. She claims we have another storm brewing. It is rare my serpent witch is wrong.

Codrin has ridden east to South Myrddin to convene with Emrys and Jonatan Pacheco. Druid and vampire leaders. He hopes to appeal to their covens through them. His wish is to show them not all warlocks want to conquer and rule.

I fear it is not enough. Codrin does not have the backing of his coven. With each passing month, more warlocks shift to the other side of the argument. It is more likely the other groups leave the warlocks to tear themselves apart from within.

It is the first time since February of 1760 that we have been without him. Only a day is gone, and his absence is a gaping hole in our world. He cannot return soon enough.

I miss the way his deep voice resonates against the stone of the castle and the tender touch of his calloused hands. I even find myself longing for the extended debates between Ness and Codrin over the most mundane subjects. Our world has always been beautiful; he simply added a new strand to our glorious prism.

Ness and I have been content and happy as a pair for so many years. It is a testament to how he changed our world that we miss him so much. Proof of how the three of us are meant to be a triad, one connected on the deepest level.

The ravens have moved on. We had months and months of them cawing at us as though we were too foolish to grasp their message. Somehow, I find their absence more concerning than their presence.

Speaking of fell omens, Bram has paid us a visit. For once, he intends not to add to the chaos. He is content in his lighthouse on the coast near South Myrddin.

I am perplexed. In all the time I have known him, Bram has always been the first fae to interfere in a conflict. He thrives on the energy of chaos.

It adds another depth to my concern. If the song-bird of strife refuses to hold a note, what is on the horizon for us? Has he noticed something I have not?

If so, what?

Two days have passed since I penned the above. Codrin's return has been far more exciting than expected, but not in a pleasant way. I am distressed by the cowardly attack that happened on his journey home.

It is Emrys who brought him to us. He has been waylaid on the road. His injuries are thankfully not life-threatening.

Codrin has no memory of his attackers. All he recalls is travelling on his stallion, a creature with whom he has a close kinship. His next memory is of waking to Emrys murmuring in some unknown language above him. His horse is nowhere to be seen.

Is it his family's enemies finally hunting him down? Or has a rogue warlock decided he is an impediment? Or is it someone else entirely? We are closing the castle to visitors, not that we have many. Emrys has kindly added to the layers of protection around us.

Ancient druids are not ones to trifle with. I have my suspicions about Emrys, he who has gone by many a name.

His wee village of foundlings will no doubt remain untouched. Only a fool will test his temper. He is a quiet, gentle man who, when provoked, will set the world ablaze to protect others.

For now, Codrin rests and heals. Ness has hunted through her family grimoire for healing poultices and tinctures. Many cauldrons have been bubbling away for hours. She will not settle until she has done something to restore him to health.

He will recover. I have tried to soothe her nerves. It is a fruitless endeavour.

My hours are spent watching them both. Codrin sleeps fitfully in a healing rest; Emrys assures us he will come out of it. Ness mostly frets over his still form.

She struggles to keep her thoughts from spiralling ever downward into potential tragedies that may or may not come to fruition. Her nerves have always been plagued thus. I can only be persistent with my reminders that all is well.

He will, as I have stated repeatedly, recover his strength. Her fears are unfounded but based out of love. I know it takes time for her to calm herself.

Emrys is, in all honesty, more concerned about the warlocks. The vampires have cut off communication with them. His strained relationship with Jonatan Pacheco has become untenable, not a quagmire I want to delve into.

The wind has picked up. Ness's predicted storm is on the horizon. We have stocked wood for the fires to carry us through the next few days.

I must finish this up and go find Ness. She is working herself into a state. We are all going to need our strength for the coming troubles.

And there will be troubles, of that I have no doubt.

While there is no proof of who is responsible for Codrin's injuries, I am not naïve enough to miss the implications. We are safe within the castle grounds. Outside them? It is a whole other story.

We, or Codrin specifically, are a stumbling block to the warlocks who crave power. They will try again. We can attempt to fight, for we cannot remain inside the castle for an eternity, or it is time for a journey to the fae realm.

I am unsure what the right path is. The safest is another matter. Nothing can touch us if we cross over. What is the correct decision for all three of us?

Only time will tell.

And I am afraid there is precious little of it left.

JOURNAL ENTRY

MARCH 1761

One last fleeting frost,
One brief flash of the sun.
All our hopes for spring,
As our days grow long.
~Ness MacDougal

There are no bright flowers budding in our gardens. Spring has yet to begin. It is barren, cold, and damp. A fitting mood for the events of the past week.

Communications between the warlocks and all other covens, families, and creatures have come to an abrupt halt. Those within their ranks who disagree have either fled voluntarily or been culled if they chose to fight.

Codrin's heart is broken over how far they have fallen. If they persist, they may find themselves exiled from Scotland or, at the very least, the Highlands. The king is already making noise in the south about ending the turmoil with his own forces.

For the most part, the king and queen are content to leave the Highlands well enough alone. It has always been closest to the fae, lending a power and protection the rest of the isles does not have. The warlock unrest, however, might tempt the royal family to turn their gaze north—something they have not done in many a year.

The royal family are a loyal yet insular group. A long line of canine shifters who claim faery ancestry from their Welsh line. They date their family back to the eleventh century or so.

I am, as always, baffled by how shifters of a small canine variety have managed to hold the throne for centuries. I am amused by it. One cannot argue with their tenacity in holding on to power. It is a pity they never attempted to quash the warlocks before their trouble strayed into our borders.

A pity or a mercy?

I cannot decide.

Emrys has hinted at the idea of the vampires, druids, and witches coming together to set boundaries on the warlocks—or to disband their council. It will certainly hamper their efforts to take control if nothing else.

It is rare for a council or coven to be affected by those outside it. An age ago, I remember the Unseelie Court being disbanded by the seelies when it went completely wild with power. It is the reason so many returned to the fae realm.

If it happens here, it will be a stain on all warlocks across the world.

Unfortunately, we have more pressing concerns.

In truth, I am delaying writing of the day's events. The fighting came to our boundaries. We are safe within the castle. They are unable to cause damage to the walls; they are like small children kicking at a boulder.

They want Codrin. He believes they fear others will rally to him as a descendant of an ancient noble line of warlocks. He is not so sure, given that his family has been exiled and most are no longer with the living. I am not eager to test the logic of those attempting to flush us out of Castle MacDougal.

Though it is unlikely they can assail the walls, we will eventually run out of food and firewood. We are cut off from food sources on the land surrounding us, though the remnants of our winter stores can carry us a while further.

Winter has not wholly released us from its icy grip. I cannot imagine those camping outside the gates will linger forever. It is undoubtedly a fool's errand to bash repeatedly against the same immovable stone again and again.

We refuse to hand Codrin out like some sacrificial lamb. It will not give the warlocks what they want. His absence will only hasten their end.

Emrys and Bram have visited us. They travel the ley lines directly into the castle walls. I am grateful the warlocks have no similar access—no greater connection to the earth around us.

Their magic is decay and chaos. Their rituals, potions, and words tread the thinnest of lines into the forbidden. It is that which keeps them from the purest link to the power available to us.

Emrys has spoken with the other druid leaders throughout the world. A rare meeting of their council. They intend to intervene if only to enforce balance and peace.

Druids are always harping on about balance in the world. It is easy to see their point in light of recent events. I worry they are moving far too slowly.

Bram has decided to remain in South Myrddin at least until the warlock problem is resolved. He is attached to the foundling. Though it is not usually in a fae's nature to be so connected to mortal beings, he and I appear to be exceptions. Perhaps the foundlings are as important to him as my loves are to me. The beings who keep us tethered to this realm when it is far less comfortable here than our true home would be.

Emrys has a better grasp of the motives of our attackers. The warlocks wanting to end Codrin's family line is only part of their plan. They also intend to lay claim to the castle and the MacDougal grimoire.

Despite our closeness, I have never held the famed book. It dates back hundreds of years. Recipes, rituals, enchantments, and tales. It is the life work of many generations of Ness's family.

A grimoire has always been a coveted thing. Sacred even. One does not touch another's. It should not be asked.

Emrys believes the warlocks think a particular ritual is hidden within the grimoire's pages. He is hearing whispers but nothing specific. It is becoming apparent that they will not stop with Codrin.

They want us all dead. We cannot fight back if we are gone. They can get their hands on what is ours without issue.

We will fight if we remain.

I am not wholly certain of our success. The vampires and druids are nowhere near ready to take on a threat like the warlocks. They are far more organised than any of us realised. The danger is greater than even Emrys predicted.

I am comforted by the knowledge that we are together.

Together.

And we can flee if we must. I can easily get a portal open to the fae realm. It is making the decision that remains the hardest part.

My hope is we do so before it is too late.

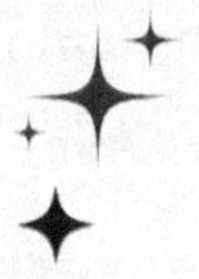

JOURNAL ENTRY

APRIL 1761

I bid farewell to my land,
With nought more than a wave of the
    hand.
Gone before they scale the walls,
We shall reconvene in the fae's hallowed
    halls.
~Ness MacDougal

Emrys has snuck into Castle MacDougal once again in the cover of darkness. For weeks, we have done nothing but hide from the world. He worries we will have to either confront the warlocks or flee.

Neither are ideal choices. The druids and vampires are not prepared to take on the warlocks. Emrys suggests a strategic retreat to the fae realm. An easy decision for me, since I can travel with relative ease between both worlds. It is not so simple for Codrin and Ness. It is a more complicated matter for my beloveds.

I will not leave them.

I cannot.

My heart rebels at even the thought. Our fates are far too intertwined. What happens to one will affect us all.

Bram has come with Emrys. He also suggests a jaunt to the court. His recommendation is for a dramatic escape. I shudder to think what he considers chaotic enough to suffice as a distraction.

However, it is not easy to leave behind one's home and legacy. Ness and Codrin are the last of their lines. If we go, their lines will come to an end.

Ness is who I worry about most. The castle, the loch, the land—it is all that remains of her family. She has always been proud of being a MacDougal. The grimoire can travel easily with her, but not the rest.

I am loath to take her away from it despite my own longing to return home. There is so much beauty to show my loves. Bram assures me that my little place within the starlight forest still stands. My family have taken care of it in my absence.

It can easily be our refuge from the coming storm. Ness has clung to the hope that they will give up. I believe even she begins to see they will not.

The warlocks have a prize within their grasp, at

least in their minds. They will not be easily persuaded to cease their attempts. There is no army to stop them, not yet.

Emrys believes it will be a month before the druids and vampires are ready to intervene. We do not have weeks. Days? Hours? We must act now.

We can, in theory, travel the ley to another part of the Highlands. It is a temporary solution. They will eventually find us. A life spent fleeing and fearing the shadows is no existence at all.

With Emrys's emphatic advice, we have to make a decision. Codrin, after an hour alone, is all for the fae realm. He says there is nothing in his life but us, so where we go, he follows.

Ness has been silent much of the day. She sits in what was once her grandfather's study and his father's before him. It houses a family tapestry dating back centuries, along with a host of books and other heirlooms.

We have left her to her thoughts. Neither of us wishes to pressure her. It is no easy thing to travel to another realm. No matter what happens, she must reach this conclusion on her own.

Emrys remains with us, not wishing to leave while decisions have yet to be made. We may require his assistance. We will find our path out no matter how dark the day grows.

It is close to midnight when Ness finally leaves the study. My heart aches for her. Her eyes are swollen and red. She actively scrubs the remnants of tears from her face.

She has wrestled over our options. If we leave, it is saying goodbye to her family's ancestral land. It is no easy choice for her.

With an obviously heavy heart, Ness has come to the same conclusion as Codrin. We will flee the castle—and the Highlands. The fae realm is the path of least resistance, the one which is guaranteed to end with us all living.

Our decision is made. The hour approaches for me to take my lovers home. Emrys will provide a distraction, giving us enough time to travel to a spot more favourable to open the portal.

The last few hours in Castle MacDougal are a whirlwind of activity. Ness knows we can only take what we can carry. She refuses to leave anything the warlocks may find useful; Emrys has promised to ensure they find nothing to steal.

He has been evasive when questioned about his plans. I have my suspicions. Ness needs not know there will be no castle remaining after our escape, only rubble to sift through.

I understand his reasons. If all that is left of Castle MacDougal are smouldering remains, it is possible the warlocks will believe us all dead. It will put an end to their search for us, distracting them for enough time for the druids and vampires to hopefully shore up their own forces.

A calm sort of chaos descends on us. Codrin has focused on the necessities. Items that may make our initial days easier, along with clothes, have all gone into a chest that he can carry. The fae realm is not barren by any means, but it is better than leaving things to rot here. Ness turns her attention to irreplaceable family heirlooms—the grimoire, a miniature version of the tapestry, her mother's necklace and her father's signet ring, and a few rare books and a ritual athame.

My belongings fit easily within the knapsack I had when I came to the Highlands over a century ago. Clothes, my writings, and a handful of books and keepsakes. I have always travelled light.

With Emrys and Bram's assistance, we make our way to a spot closer to South Myrddin. It is in a grove of trees, a hidden place behind a massive boulder. It has been so long that it takes me a moment to open the portal.

I can hear home calling to me. I am sad for my loves —for their regrets and fears. But I have none of my own. My heart sings as I lead us through to our next adventure.

Light beckons. We step from the dry, cold ground, and seconds later, our feet touch soft, plush grass. A gentle breeze jostles the leaves of the forest behind us.

The world we left is on the edge of spring, while the fae realm is perpetually a riot of colour. I will need to present the three of us to the court. It can wait until we have found my home and settled ourselves.

My beloveds fall silent in awe of the beauty surrounding them. For the first time, I see my home through another's eyes. Words fail me, for I am not the poet that my Ness is.

As luck would have it, the portal is but a few minutes' walk from the path leading to my cottage. The little stone walls surrounding it are still standing. My garden has been well-loved; I imagine my mother is the culprit. She has always adored tending to a wild patch of flowers and herbs.

Vines wind their way up the stone cottage. The roof is covered in soft moss, allowing it to blend in with the canopy of trees overhead. I can see the blue door is as bright as ever, likely redone in my absence.

A basket sits by the door with a note. My father informs me that he has foreseen our arrival. The Unseelie Court expects our attendance on the morrow —as does my family. The latter, I assume, will be far more enjoyable than the former.

My loves hesitantly follow me inside the cottage. Its

warmth beckons us in as though it wishes to envelop us in a healing comfort.

I am not naïve enough to believe this leap into the unknown will be without its own troubles. But we are alive and safe. They cannot reach us here. We have a chance to build our future—our lives together for as long as we wish.

We have found the courage to grasp our future.

I am at peace.

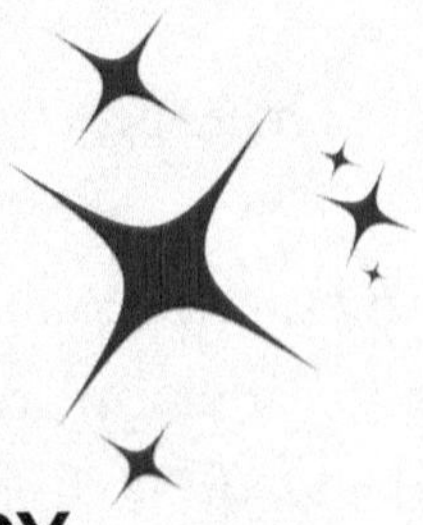

JOURNAL ENTRY

APRIL 1879

My loves brought me joy,
Though my heart is rent in two.
I have left my home behind,
But my loves are worth all I endure.
~Ness MacDougal

Over a hundred years have flown by since our escape. Ness is the one who suggested my sojourn to the Highlands. She wants to know how the world has changed without us.

And it is greatly altered.

Another age is upon us. The nineteenth century has brought industry to the Highlands and the world. It appears to be both a boon and a curse from all accounts. I have no intention of lingering long enough to determine which.

I have brought with me a bouquet of flowers I gathered to symbolise sorrow and love in equal measure, an homage to the land where we lived for so long. It is only after I place them by the loch that I truly see the castle for the first time in an aeon.

It is a mere relic of what had stood for centuries. A few walls are all that remain. The skeleton of a home. All of its flesh and blood is gone, not enough for even ghosts to haunt. I am glad Ness is not here to see the crumbling remnants of her ancestral castle.

A sign now stands by the water—Loch Ness. There are local rumours of a monster hidden in the waters. A slippery serpentlike creature. None can say for sure who saw the beast first or what she is.

Nessie.

My Ness will find this highly amusing. A mythical sea monster in her loch has now been named after her. I sense the mischief-making skills of either Bram or Emrys. They have clearly turned us into a mysterious bit of folklore.

A person walking nearby informs me flowers are left each year. The message of the bouquet is clear to me—everlasting love, longing, and loss are the meaning of the individual flowers. It has only fed rumours about a brokenhearted witch and a scandalous love affair. While we have left this world behind, it has clearly not been allowed to forget us in an absurdly amusing way.

As I clamber through what was once a castle, I am struck by so many bittersweet memories. It is almost impossible to reconcile where I know rooms once stood to the rubble at my feet.

I slip here and there on the slick stone. Amusement fades into sadness at the destruction. Nothing really is left.

Nothing of worth to bring home to my loves. A spare bit of stone? A crumbling splinter of what once was a mighty beam? Time has begun to wither away even the barest of recognisable traces.

What will remain in another hundred?

A hint of dust?

I sense his presence long before I turn to see him. Emrys appears as if out of the mist. His beard and hair are slightly longer and greyer than when we last met. An air of sadness hovers around him as our eyes meet.

Despite a century having flown by, his memories of that night are etched in stone. Initially, he does not speak of our flight to the fae or the immense magic spent dragging down the castle. He mentions that the warlocks are gone; only one or two remain in Scotland, and none wish to further invite the collective wrath of Emrys, Bram, and the vampires. Peace has remained since our escape.

Emrys has one last surprise for me—a painting of the castle in all its original glory. It is familiar to me, as it once hung in the study and was done by Ness's great-grandfather. Knowing I would likely return one day, it is one of the few things he saved.

I am grateful for it, though it is possible I will never come again. It is too painful to be away from my loves. There is nothing in this world I wish to see.

Our flight to the fae did save us. Emrys tells me of the warlock ritual they discovered. It would have brought the walls down on us before our escape, knowledge which solidifies my belief that we made the right decision.

The warlocks did turn their gaze towards South Myrddin—a fatal and final mistake.

His village thrives. More and more foundlings find their way there. It does my spirit good to see his pure joy and deep determination to build a safe home for those who have none. He has done well.

I share my own happiness with him. Our cottage in the forest is full of light, laughter, and love. In many ways, we have created our own much smaller version of South Myrddin in the fae realm. We have gathered others to us, finding a home that helps us flourish.

Nothing remains to be said. Our paths may never cross again. I wish Emrys well and offer my blessing of protection over his foundlings. A final sacrifice of magic, one well worth the minuscule cost of a few days of exhaustion.

My journey back to the portal seems far longer than it should be. I walk faster, anxious to return to my beloveds. I am glad I came, but I am beyond ready to return.

I am at peace.

Our choice to flee, made in a state of panic, has been the best decision. We are happy. There is so much love in our world.

We are content.

FEBRUARY 10, 2024
TERESA

"What are we looking for?" Teresa trudged behind Hyde. Her vampire partner had dragged them out to Loch Ness and the remnants of Castle MacDougal. "Love? Are you listening?"

"No." Hyde was intently focused on the castle ahead of them. "Sorry. Yes. I heard you. The treasure hunter found the journal buried not far from the loch."

"You mean archaeologist?"

"Same difference." Hyde shrugged. They clambered over a section of what had once been a castle wall. "I think there's more here."

"Why?"

"Intuition? Of the vampire variety?"

Teresa narrowed her eyes, staring at Hyde for a moment. The slight monotone delivery made it hard to

know if they were being serious. "Is it different from witch intuition?"

"Fewer herbs and spells." Hyde laughed when Teresa flicked a tiny speck of stone at them. "I don't know why, Resa. I just can't help thinking there's something more here for us to find."

"Did you ask Emrys or Bram again?"

"Both. They claim to not know anything. It was... odd." Hyde kicked a rock, launching it far across the rippling water. "Maybe Morag put a geas on their story on her last trip to the Highlands? Making sure they would forget or not be able to speak about it? A powerful fae should be capable of that, right?"

Ever since translating the journal, Hyde had only grown more fascinated by the lore of Nessie. They'd peppered Emrys and Bram with questions, which went unanswered. It was strange.

"Would someone be able to put a geas on either of them?" Teresa had never dabbled in that form of magic —to force a person to not speak on a subject. She'd known witches who had. It was a tricky art to master, particularly when the two involved were so powerful in their own right. "What if they were willing?"

"But why?"

"Maybe Bram and Emrys wanted to protect the three lovers' peace and safety?"

"Theoretically, it's possible, and it would explain

Bram's interest in Ness mythology and his encouragement of my research while not seeming to know anything himself." Hyde pondered the idea for a moment. "All the mythology around Morag claims she was a powerful fae sorceress, certainly one strong enough if both Bram and Emrys were willing."

Having known Emrys for a while, Teresa had no doubts he'd willingly allow a geas if it protected others. He'd sacrifice a great deal for those he cared about.

Unsure of what to search for, Teresa followed Hyde. They picked their way through the site, finding nothing interesting besides crumbling walls. There was only an hour or so of daylight left.

A frustrated Hyde finally sat on the edge of what had once been part of the entrance. They stared across to the loch in the distance. Their disappointment was obvious to see.

Teresa hated seeing their shoulders slump. "Archaeologists aren't always successful on their first treasure hunt."

"Maybe we should've brought the furry fiends. They could've played sniffer cats for us." Hyde scratched their head for a second. Teresa wasn't entirely sure the two cats were inclined to hunt through the remnants of an old castle. "Or maybe a metal detector? Or a map?"

"In the journal, Morag mentions a grove." Teresa gestured towards trees in the distance. "We know how sacred a ritual circle is. It would be at the top of the list if I were hiding treasures. Who would go around digging it up?"

Hyde's eyes brightened and then narrowed. "What do you think we'd find under the circle in Raven Park in the village?"

"We're not digging up the village."

"Not all of it." Hyde leapt up and grasped Teresa's hand. They clambered down the rubble towards the grove in the distance. "Just by the fire."

Teresa held back a laugh. Hyde had clearly become hyper-focused on the idea of lost historical artefacts and mysteries. "We should probably wait until it's warmer outside to dig around for any extended period."

"Fair point." Hyde slowed their pace when Teresa stumbled over a patch of uneven ground. "Sorry, Resa."

"No wor—" Teresa cut herself off when they reached the small, barren copse of trees. Spring hadn't sprung quite yet, leaving them all bare. She wondered how much the area had grown in the past four hundred years or so. "We should come back in the spring to see it in all its glory. Maybe we could do a ritual of our own to celebrate them. To celebrate love."

It felt like a fitting tribute to the trio of lovers who had captured Hyde's imagination. Teresa knew exactly which one to do. She made a mental note to prepare everything for mid- to late April.

"Resa?"

She turned around to find Hyde inspecting the roots of one of the older trees. "Find something?"

"The geas." Hyde rubbed what they'd found on their trousers, then lifted a tiny bottle. They tapped their finger against the wax seal. "Have you ever broken one?"

"Never dabbled in the art of geas."

Hyde held the bottle up, allowing it to catch the last rays of the afternoon sun. "It feels like a rubber band snapping inside you."

Teresa frowned at the implication of their words. "You have personal experience with it?"

"Emrys freed me from a geas placed on me as a child." Hyde tilted the glass from side to side, watching the contents shift. "We should show this to him and Bram. It should be their choice."

"It could be connected to anyone."

"There's a part of a merlin falcon feather inside this." Hyde carefully slipped the bottle into the pocket of their coat. "It has to be connected to Emrys."

Nodding, Teresa couldn't argue with Hyde's logic.

With a new mystery to solve, they made their way

back to South Myrddin. The sun had finally begun to set as they arrived in the village, quickly making their way to Druid Lane, where Emrys lived.

"Hello, foundlings." Emrys waved from his garden as they approached. He led them into his cottage, ushering them to the table in the kitchen while he put on the kettle. "I saw the bookshop and taco truck were closed early. Did you have an adventure?"

"More of an archaeological dig." Hyde gingerly placed the centuries-old bottle on the table. "We went mucking around the woods near Loch Ness and the castle. This was hidden in the roots of a tree."

Emrys crouched down for a closer inspection. He carefully avoided touching the geas. Teresa had no doubts he'd immediately recognised what it was. "It's still sealed."

"Not my place to decide." Hyde fidgeted under the intense gaze of the druid who'd practically raised them—and most of the foundlings in the village. "The geas is connected to you—and maybe Bram?"

"I believe you're right."

Teresa placed a comforting hand on Hyde's shoulders. It was easy to see how much the idea bothered them. "Hyde?"

"Controlling someone's ability to speak is…." Hyde shook their head, unable to find the words to express their feelings. It was something the autistic vampire often struggled with. "I don't like this kind of magic."

"Aye. I'm not a great fan of it either. There is a difference this time, though, foundling." Emrys smiled gently at them. He stood up and reached out to draw them into a quick, comforting embrace. "Whatever is held by this geas, I willingly agreed to it. I'll honour that decision. My curiosity isn't so great that it needs to be sated at the risk of another's secrets."

Hyde grumbled under their breath for several seconds before finally nodding. "Okay."

"We'll put it back tonight. A full moon. Fortuitous timing for the resealing of a pact." Teresa helped Hyde settle back into one of the kitchen chairs. "A late Imbolc celebration of sorts."

They spent the rest of the evening preparing for their small ritual. It was almost midnight when they returned to the overgrown grove of trees near Castle MacDougal. They brought with them a feast, candles, and a blanket.

Despite the fierce wind blowing across the loch, it was calm within the shelter of the woods. They laid the blanket on the ground, setting out their feast and offerings before lighting their candles. Teresa made a small fire in what had once been the ritual bonfire for those who celebrated centuries ago.

The air was heavy. Teresa could almost feel the

weight of forgotten memories around them. She heard the murmurs of rituals past on the wind.

Hyde reached for the bottle after they finished their feast. They returned it to the tree roots, methodically ensuring it was well hidden. "We'll remember them."

"We will."

Hyde returned to sit beside Teresa on the blanket. They leaned their head against her shoulder. "There was a scrap of parchment between the pages of the journal. Another of Ness's unfinished poems."

"Read it to me?"

> With magic woven through the veil,
> Sweet Morag keeps us whole and hale.
> With strength and power all his own,
> Dear Codrin carries us through dangers
> > unknown.
> For my dearest loves,
> I'll wreck whole entire worlds.
> For my dearest loves
> Are worth their weight in gold.
> ~Ness MacDougal

THE END

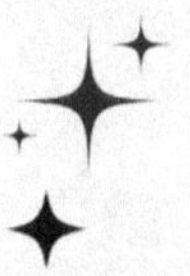

WHEY TO HIS HEART

When fated mates meet over the renovation of an old stone cottage, an introverted lion shifter and a gargoyle stonemason find themselves building a connection stone by stone. The two men battle the weather, their own doubts, and their chronic illness to find common ground. Sometimes, the universe knows just what one needs in life.

CHAPTER 1
WHEY

"Some days, Rocky, getting out of bed just isn't worth it." Whey lifted his little grey hamster off his chest and placed the creature on a pillow. "Today is going to be absolutely shite."

Whey Southcott had the misfortune of inheriting the gargoyle side from his father and a hereditary genetic abnormality from his mother. As a result, he suffered from a unique form of fibromyalgia that worsened whenever he dared shift into his stone form. He avoided it as much as possible.

Some days, Whey had no issues at all. He ran his stonemasonry business and volunteered as a local paramedic. Other times, he simply couldn't get out of bed because of how debilitating it was.

The pain tended to lessen when Whey avoided shifting to his gargoyle—a tricky thing since he had to

change periodically. It meant the chronic ache and exhaustion never went away. It was simply part of his life, and he worked around it.

With a tired groan, Whey pushed himself out of bed. He deftly plucked Rocky up and deposited him into his palatial castle. The hamster immediately disappeared into one of the many burrows.

Despite the ache in his bones, Whey had a new job and client to work with. He'd been hired to fix the stonework inside and outside an old cottage on the outskirts of Kyle of Lochalsh. It was on the north side of the village,

The project was for someone new to the area—a lion shifter. Ntare Morgan. He'd been told it was pronounced like Atari with an N at the start and an "ay" at the end. He'd sounded nice enough, and Whey appreciated a client who trusted him.

Old cottages tended to be tricky restorations, but he enjoyed the challenge. He often had ideas for what to do. It was always better when the owner allowed him to make decisions.

Stonemasonry was in his blood, literally and figuratively. The gargoyles in his family had always worked with their hands. The business went back centuries. One of his ancestors had even helped build Castle MacDougal.

For all their storied history, though, Whey was the

only living Southcott in Scotland. Gargoyle clans were rare. No other family claimed the Highlands as home. In some ways, it was good he was an introvert and preferred to keep to himself; otherwise, he might have been lonely.

Still, for all his being by himself, he sometimes missed family. Whey had a few friends, mostly amongst the druids. It kept him from leading a truly hermit-like existence. Aside from helping patients as a paramedic, he avoided people whenever possible. That was more than enough for him.

Whey headed into the bathroom and stared blearily at his reflection in the mirror. *C'mon. Wake up. Stones won't put themselves together.*

With his silver hair, stormy grey eyes, and pale, almost ashen tone to his skin, Whey bore more than a slight resemblance to his gargoyle form. A softer version—a fragile one. The pain made him more breakable than most of his kind.

After finishing up his breakfast, Whey checked on Rocky to make sure his wee friend had food, water, and all of his needs met. He grabbed his coat and headed outside, shivering when a blast of wind hit him. "Sodding weather."

Snow was imminent. He had a feeling the next few days would be rough. Cold and damp weather tended to exacerbate his fibromyalgia.

Making his way to the shed, Whey grabbed the supplies he'd need. He loaded up his work van and placed his backpack in the front seat. It held snacks, his laptop, and a large coffee-filled thermos—always a necessity for him.

The first days on a site were always challenging. Whey could be taciturn by nature. Some clients found him hard to figure out. It didn't affect his ability to coerce stones into doing what he wanted.

Whey sat in his van for several minutes. He sensed the deep ache in his bones creeping up on him. "Not today. I *need* it to be a good day."

After several more minutes, Whey eventually gathered the energy to start the van. The journey to the cottage wasn't a long one. The van squeezed between the hedgerows on the narrow lane leading away from the village to the little wooded area on the top of a hill. It overlooked the inlet on the west side of Kyle of Lochalsh.

The cottage had belonged to a witch for ages, then sat empty for almost a century before his new client bought it. He was looking forward to getting started.

The new owner was a food vlogger. Whey had no idea what a food vlogger did since he rarely went online. His druid friend Hamish joked he was stuck in the Stone Age.

Suddenly, Whey felt his gargoyle practically roaring

in his mind. He just barely managed to avoid shifting in the van. It hurt to deny himself.

Once he'd pulled off the road, Whey got out of the van. He stalked to the edge of the shoreline and peered across the water. It was a beautiful, crisp morning.

Damp and cold.

The wind whipped around him. His gargoyle ached to be released. He longed to stomp around and soar into the sky, but he couldn't. Every single transformation took a massive toll on his body. It had been a crushing blow when he'd first learned it. A gargoyle who couldn't gargoyle.

With one last longing look towards the turbulent sea, Whey returned to the van and set off down the lane. It had been a while since he'd been there to assess the cottage in person. The building itself hadn't changed, but he could see progress had been made in clearing out the garden.

Ntare had mentioned wanting to create a lush, edible garden. The overgrown mess of weeds and dead flora had been removed. Off to one side, Whey spotted a collection of material for raised beds along with a greenhouse and shed. He wondered if his new client intended to build them himself.

It was definitely outside the scope of what Whey usually did. He'd been quite firm when they'd gone over the contract. Stone was his preferred medium. All of the damaged outer and inner walls could be dealt with. The rest was someone else's problem, though he had made a few suggestions for other local contractors.

In the Highlands, there was a close-knit community of craftspeople. They frequently referred clients back and forth between one another. Most projects in their area involved older cottages and estates, which required a higher level of expertise than a modern home might.

Whey climbed out of the van. He went around to the back, opening the doors and taking a second to ensure he'd brought everything necessary for the tenth time. He heard footsteps, then a throat being cleared, so he turned to greet his client over his shoulder. "Morning."

"Hello."

Whey closed one of the back doors and faced his client. He'd forgotten how stunningly attractive the man was—not that he usually noticed those things. It wasn't professional. *Remember Hamish's advice: Be nice, not grumpy.* "Morning."

You just said that, you numpty.

"Hello," Ntare repeated with the slightest of grins. "Are you still wanting to start outside, or do you want to come inside, given the weather?"

"Inside." Whey grunted the word as if it offended

him. *That's not being nice.* He sighed to himself. "I should get started. Stones won't fix themselves."

Ntare turned glowing amber eyes in his direction. They stood in stark contrast to his black skin, carefully trimmed beard, and hair. He cleared his throat again when Whey stared at him for long enough for the silence to become awkward. "How about we step inside? Winter definitely gets colder here than in Cornwall."

"Fair enough." Whey grabbed the folder with the plans, along with one of his tool bags. He'd come back for the rest. "Show me where you'd like to start. I know some of the inner and outer walls are in worse shape than others. I'd like to shore things up to ensure we don't lose any more than absolutely necessary."

"The kitchen walls have the most damage. Perhaps starting there?" Ntare led the way into the cottage. "I cleared everything out. The carpenter you recommended came in last week to remove all the cabinets. Once the stonework is finished, he'll be back to replace them."

"Perfect." Whey moved into the space. Aside from the hob and a fridge, it had been stripped bare of everything. He took a deep breath, pushing his mind to focus on the job, not the attractive client. "I'll get started now."

"Excellent."

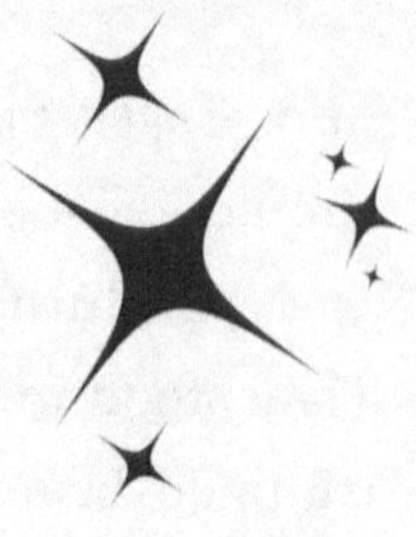

CHAPTER 2
NTARE

OH. HELLO AGAIN. Ntare had heard the saying—tall, dark, and handsome. His stonemason was tall, brooding, and all shades of grey. He'd watched Whey park and get out of his van for a moment, trying to settle his stomach before heading outside to greet him.

The awkward hellos had been sweet. Ntare sternly warned himself not to get attached to his contractor. The man was there to build his walls without any hint or hope of romance.

Maybe he'd read too many novels. His work as a food vlogger meant he had plenty of time to spend at home, much of which was spent cooking, reading, or curled up in pain from his constant stomach issues. It was ironic how much he loved food when it gave him no end of trouble.

His lion itched to leap out of his skin. Another

predator in his space. Whey Southcott smelled of pain, stone, and storms. What manner of being was he?

A gargoyle?

Those were rare. He'd never met one himself. His contractor smelled like Ntare imagined a being made of stone might.

Whey paused when low croaking was heard from further in the cottage. "A new form of toad?"

"My birds."

"You have birds?"

"Two great eared nightjars. They… found me." Ntare fidgeted uneasily. He grasped a ball of yarn from the counter, picking at one of the threads. "Quite vocal when they want to be."

"A nightjar?" Whey set his tools down and then crouched to open one of the bags. "What sort of feathered beastie is that?"

"They're not native to Scotland. They found me when I was travelling through India years ago and refused to leave." Ntare had always been adamant about not having a pet or familiar. "They were insistent."

For much of his life, Ntare had greatly feared smaller creatures, not because they might harm him but the reverse. As a child, he'd developed an irrational fear of accidentally eating one while in his lion form. Something he hadn't been able to shake even after Wagu and Fear came into his life.

It had been something that grew legs and turned into a fully-fledged phobia. Then two dragon-shaped birds swooped into his world; they'd changed everything. He hadn't stood a chance against their stubbornness.

The names had been partially a joke—a way to cope with his phobia. Fear had been the first nightjar to insistently follow him around. Wagu had been the second. Neither feathered menace had shown an ounce of concern about him as a human or lion.

Their names had been a constant source of amusement for his friends. Fear had been named thus because of his own phobias regarding pets and the lack of terror when Ntare had first turned into a lion. Wagu had simply been called that since it was his cooking obsession at the time. Nightjars were rather large birds. They'd found him while he'd been travelling Coimbatore in Tamil Nadu, India. Their long ear tufts and barred tails gave them a distinct appearance that vaguely resembled a dragon.

"Will the dust bother them?"

"Nsia will pick them up in about an hour." Ntare glanced at his watch, realising more time had passed than he'd thought. "Not an hour, in about ten minutes."

"Perfect. I'll use the time to finish prepping the room." Whey continued digging through his tool kit. "Dust and noise probably aren't good for their delicate lungs."

Ntare nodded his agreement. "You're not wrong."

"You know the Barbiers?"

"Hmm? Yes. They are the sisters of my soul." He had known the twin naiads for most of his life. "Our mothers were from the same village in Rwanda, and our fathers hale from the same region in France, though mine moved to Cornwall when he was quite young."

"They told you about the cottage?"

"They did." Ntare had been adrift when the twins had reached out to him. "They thought I'd find peace here. They love South Myrddin but knew I'd feel claustrophobic there, so this was a better solution."

Nsia and Zuri Barbier had lived in the village since they were twins when their parents passed away in a tragic accident. The rest of their family had abandoned them, leaving them with little choice.

When Ntare made a comment about wanting a change of pace, the twins immediately mentioned a cottage on the edge of a wooded copse near an inlet. It was close enough to Kyle of Lochalsh for it not to be too inconvenient but far enough away to provide him the space he wanted.

Travelling had been good for him. It forced him to expand his horizons when it came to cooking and other aspects of life. Yet the constant moving had begun to weigh heavily on his spirit.

His mother had always warned him that he couldn't avoid putting down roots forever. A lion needed stability and territory. She hadn't been entirely wrong.

The older Ntare grew, the more he found himself veering away from life on the go. A sharp contrast to his late teens and early twenties when being a "lone wolf" ever moving had been his default. Wanderlust had flowed through his veins; his feet never wanted to be still.

Part of his desire to find a home once and for all was the health problems he'd developed. Doctors had taken forever to finally suggest he had Irritable Bowel Syndrome, or IBS. It had been disheartening when they'd explained that not enough information was known about it, nor did they have a solid plan to alleviate the problem.

A few medications had been suggested, along with experimenting with diet changes. Ntare had always enjoyed cooking, so he'd thrown himself even more into his love of food. It led to him developing a new career as a food vlogger and writer.

Ntare realised the quiet in the cottage had grown a

little loud. He hadn't spoken in several long minutes, standing in the middle of the kitchen while Whey worked.

Sod it. I can't just stay quiet forever. Can I leave? Would he notice?

The awkward silence filled the cottage like a lead balloon, one punctured only occasionally by the clang of Whey's tools or one of the birds croaking or chirping. Ntare had never been more relieved for a distraction than when he'd heard a vehicle pull up outside; his keen hearing told him Nsia had arrived.

Ntare waited for the hurricane of madness his friend often brought with her. "Door is open."

"Here, kitty, kitty." She knocked on the door before yanking it open. "Hello."

"Nsia." Ntare sighed while studiously avoiding glancing at Whey. "I'm not a cat."

"Technically, you are," she teased. Her gaze darted towards the well-built stonemason. "You are the king of the felines."

"Okay… trout."

"First of all, I am *not* a fish." Nsia flicked her long braids over her shoulder and sniffed derisively. "I *am* a naiad."

"Same difference." Ntare met her glare with one of his own before they both dissolved into giggles. "Hello, *mon amie.*"

"Yeah, yeah, don't bust out the French that neither of us ever uses to get on my good side." She nudged him gently on his arm and leaned in closer, dropping her voice to a whisper. "Isn't he delicious? All brooding with his silver hair and grey eyes and muscles."

"Unlike the stone in my hands, I have functioning ears." Whey interrupted their whispered gossip session about him, much to Ntare's embarrassment. "Are the birds being removed at some point? I can't start removing the damaged parts of the wall until they are."

"Right. We'll do that." Nsia grabbed Ntare by the arm and dragged him out of the kitchen. She was definitely laughing at him. "Sorry."

"Are you?" He ignored her snickering and opened the bedroom door. Fear and Wagu immediately perked up. They flew over to land on his shoulders; he grunted at the combined weight. "Auntie Nsia is taking you to her place for a few days. There will be plenty of fresh fish for you to chase down. Be good for her."

The two birds nodded solemnly, then flew over to perch on her shoulders. Ntare gathered up a few things, shoving them into a bag. Nsia was still eyeing her new companions warily.

"Sometimes I wonder if these two aren't one of your ancient ancestors reincarnated. Never seen birds so in tune with their person." She had a healthy respect for the nightjars. "Just let us know if you need anything."

"I'll be fine."

"He is handsome, though."

"Nsia. Go away now." He sighed at his old friend, who remained unmoved by his ire. "Please?"

"Settle your fur, lion." She chirped at the two birds and continued out of the bedroom and then cottage.

To his great relief, Nsia left with his feathered friends without further embarrassing him. He helped her get them comfortably situated into her Range Rover and watched her drive off. It was hard to see Fear and Wagu leave for a few days, even though he knew it would be safer for them.

A few snowflakes drifted into his face. Ntare batted them away. It had been a while since he'd experienced a cold winter; he'd travelled through warmer places during the year's cooler months.

He swatted at another flake, dropping his hand a second later. Feline instincts were hard to ignore, no matter how hard he tried.

You are not a house cat. Stop it.

Pep talk over, and he stalked back to the cottage and ignored the siren call of falling flakes.

One year, for his birthday, the Barbier twins had sent him a toy mouse filled with catnip. Ntare had played more enthusiastically with it than he'd ever admit to them. He kept it hidden with several other treasures in the bottom of a chest; no one ever needed to know he played with it.

Just him—and the birds.

And they always kept his secrets.

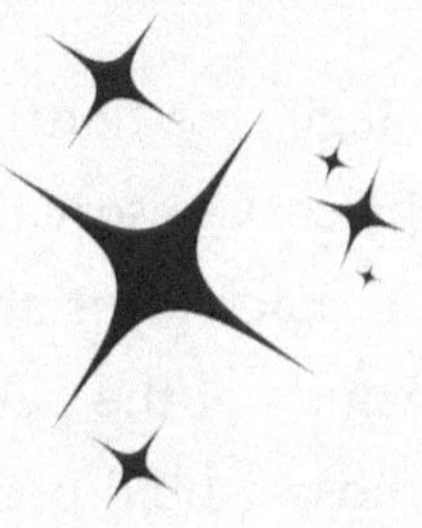

CHAPTER 3
WHEY

WHEY DIDN'T NEED TO LOOK OUTSIDE TO KNOW SNOW had started to fall. He sensed it deep in his bones. *I should've stayed in bed. This is going to be a nightmare of a day.*

The jolts of pain weren't sharp. They throbbed, a low level of ache that refused to fade away.

He gritted his teeth and focused on the task at hand. *One stone at a time.* His chronic pain made him feel brittle in temper and body. One sharp hammer strike would shatter his stones.

With pure stubbornness, Whey pushed it out of his mind. He had to carefully remove the damaged parts of the walls while shoring up and checking the rest. It wouldn't do to waste materials if it wasn't necessary.

Being a stonemason was akin to surgery at this

stage. He had to delicately excise the decay piece by piece. Conservation mattered.

Each part told him a story. Whey imagined the hands of the person who built the cottage. The lives of those who'd been sheltered within its walls. His ancestors had considered stone to be sacred. Whey had never been one for religious or spiritual beliefs, but he did have a kinship with it. Maybe that's what they'd meant.

The lines of lime mortar were the veins of the cottage's body. His family had a specific blend that held strong and lasted better than any modern cement. He swore by it.

With meticulous precision, Whey chiselled away at the old mortar. He preserved any stones he could repurpose. His fingers trembled, which made the difficult task harder.

As minutes passed, it became clear the job couldn't start today. Pain made him want to curl up in a ball. His fingers didn't curve around the tools right, and his grip wasn't firm enough to control them.

Normally, the rhythm of a hammer against his chisel resonated deep within him. A happy melody. Each strike hit a perfect chord. Days like today were an off-key nightmare, like the shriek of a banshee.

He'd likely do more damage than good if he forced himself to work. It was better to quit and return than add days to a contract to fix any mistakes. His fibromyalgia had been the reason his contracts were all carefully worded to allow him to leave when his body refused to cooperate.

Decision made, Whey began to put his tools away. It was only going to get worse, and he had to get home before driving became impossible.

"Should I call you Whey?" Ntare returned to the cottage. They hadn't spoken much in person when negotiating the contract. He'd visited it with one of the twins since the client was still travelling. "Or do you prefer something else?"

He wanted to answer in a friendly manner, but all he managed was an angry grunt. *Shite.*

"Are you—"

"I have to go." Whey had no energy to do anything other than walk a little unsteadily out of the cottage. His strength waned. He regretted his sharp tone but couldn't summon the focus to form words. The pain had gone from an ache he could almost ignore to a burning and stabbing sensation impossible to put out of his mind. Fatigue was sure to follow. "Tomorrow. Tomorrow."

He dropped his tools in the van, barely managing to get them in the right spot. Ntare stared at him in bewilderment as Whey entered the van and started the engine. Neither of them said anything. It was a good thing, since he didn't have the energy to feign politeness. In his rearview mirror, Whey saw a puzzled Ntare watching him until he turned the corner. It had certainly not been an ideal beginning for his new contract. He hoped his client would understand when he explained later.

His journey home took an age and a half. Whey struggled with the urge to shift into his gargoyle, something that happened with every intense flare-up of his condition.

The strong desire to change often smacked headfirst into the dangers of it. He couldn't become stone. It only served to increase the intensity of his illness. The immovable object, his fibromyalgia, met the unstoppable force of his nature within his body, causing him to pay a painful price.

To his immense relief, Whey arrived home safely. He left his gear in the van and trudged into the cottage. His brain was sluggish, as if moving through a thick, gooey caramel.

Whey dug through the cabinets in his kitchen, hunting for the tincture Wilfred had prescribed and Emrys had created for him. Both druids, the former was the South Myrddin doctor and the latter dabbled with potions in his home apothecary. Whey wouldn't trust anyone else to make it for him. "Down the hatch with you."

Grimacing at the taste, Whey forced himself to swallow. He set the bottle on the counter and wandered into the living room. The burning in his body slowly abated, leaving him shivering with cold and a deep-seated ache in his bones.

Whey knelt by the hearth and started a fire. He pushed himself up with great effort. His body protested every single movement. *It's going to be one of those days.*

After checking on Rocky, Whey collapsed on the couch. He stared up at the ceiling for a while. Even with the cold, he avoided the blankets. The weight of the fabric was enough to set him off.

A squeak from the large terrarium caught his attention.

"Not a good day, Rocky." Whey twisted onto his side, curling up. "Just give me a minute."

Heat from the fire slowly filled the room. A slow wave of warmth settled over him. He closed his eyes against the pain, allowing comfort to sink into his bones. The tincture took hours to fully take effect. Once it did, sleep would come. He'd be grateful for the relief.

Whey cracked one eye open when Rocky squeaked again. "It's all going to be okay—eventually. I promise."

CHAPTER 4
NTARE

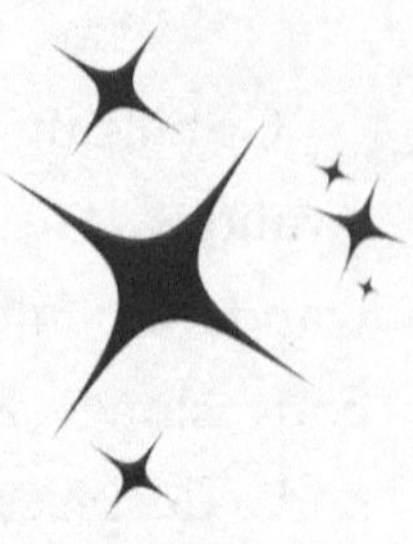

"What just happened?" Ntare hadn't moved from his spot in front of the cottage. His gaze was glued to the empty lane, where not even a cloud of dust remained from Whey's quick exit. "What *just* happened?"

He was reasonably confident he hadn't said anything to upset the man. The contract they'd worked out included a subsection about Whey's need to leave or take a day off due to a chronic illness. Something he had understood with his own difficulties.

It hadn't mentioned anything about the abrupt nature of the leaving. Ntare tried to be understanding. Pain could make even the kindest of souls a grump.

Returning to the cottage, Ntare sighed at the beginnings of the mess the kitchen would become. It was a temporary state of being but still not a pleasant one. He regretted having his birds picked up; they could've kept him company for another day or two.

A peek out the window showed the snow was falling thick and fast. A beautiful but chilly sight. Ntare supposed he should be grateful more hadn't been done in the kitchen. He could still use it.

All of the cabinets were gone, but his nonperishables were in a little cupboard off the kitchen. The refrigerator worked, as did the hob. He scrounged around until he found one of his many blends of loose-leaf tea, one meant to be calming.

The cottage didn't retain heat well. Ntare got the fire going and threw a thick blanket around himself while he waited for the kettle to heat up. He'd sip his tea and contemplate what to make of his grumpy stonemason.

Ntare shuffled over to a stack of papers on a bookshelf, hunting through them to find the contract. He scanned it for one of the qualifying clauses. "Owing to a chronic illness, the undersigned understands Whey Southcott may be late, leave early, or skip a day entirely."

Extra days had been added to their planning. Ntare hadn't really thought much about it at the time. It made far more sense now than it had when they signed it.

With suddenly at least a day to himself, Ntare

contemplated what to do with the free time. He made his tea once the kettle boiled and took a tentative sip when it had cooled sufficiently. Snow falling meant being outdoors might be an option.

His lion loved the idea. There was no one around to see him playing. Ntare's second glance out the window showed the snow had begun to stick to the ground— maybe in a couple of hours, he'd allow himself to play outside.

When Zuri messaged him in the early afternoon, Ntare mistakenly mentioned Whey's unexpected absence. The following silence was alarming. He sighed before going to put the kettle on, knowing he'd soon have visitors of the naiad variety.

True to his expectations, a knock sounded not fifteen minutes later. Ntare had tea and a tray of treats waiting for them. The twins crashed into the cottage with all the calm of a category-five hurricane.

"What did he do?"

"We'll flail him alive."

Ntare rolled his eyes at their dramatics, though he appreciated their ire on his behalf. "You both need to take a deep breath. You're impossible to understand when you're talking over each other. Also, no knives are required. He was a bit abrupt and grumpy, though if he has some sort of chronic illness, it might've been because of pain."

"Still rude," Zuri grumbled around a mouthful of a spiced coconut biscuit. "We'll check on him."

"I wish you wouldn't." Ntare could see from the stubborn set of their jaws that there would be no talking them out of it. "Be nice to him."

"We'll be as nice as the situation requires." Zuri snatched up the last of the coconut biscuits.

"We'll talk to him." Nsia gave her twin a sharp nod. "Today."

Ntare regretted mentioning it to them at all. A slight possible misunderstanding had likely just become a much larger issue. "I'd rather—"

"We'll have a friendly wee chat with him. Make sure he's okay." Nsia patted his arm before setting down her cup of tea. "Best be off. Don't want to get trapped by snow."

They said their goodbyes and left as quickly and chaotically as they'd come. Ntare scrubbed his hand across his face. There wasn't much to be done but hope they didn't chase off his stonemason.

Ntare cleared up the tea things and then went to stand by one of the living room windows. A soft blanket of snow covered just about everything. There was maybe an hour or two of daylight left. He rubbed his hand over his chest when his lion rumbled within him. "Yes, yes. We'll go play in the fluffy white stuff while no one's watching."

After stepping outside and changing into his lion, Ntare shook himself for a second. There was always a point during the shift when his bones felt misaligned. He gave his body a moment to settle.

A flake dropped on his nose. Ntare told himself to resist. *I am a lion. A majestic creature. Some might say an apex predator.* A second flake proved impossible to ignore—he leapt forward. He skidded across the icy ground, rolling a few times before coming to a stop. He raced around the grove of trees near his cottage, slipping and sliding at times.

Ntare allowed himself the freedom and joy to frolic around in the snow, something he couldn't remember ever doing. He hadn't enjoyed a proper winter very often in his life. As the snow fell thicker and faster, he tilted his head back and roared with delight. *Maybe I haven't made a mistake by moving up here to the wilds of the Highlands.*

When Ntare began to shiver despite his thick coat of fur, he made the journey back to the cottage. He shook himself violently, trying to get the snow and damp off him before returning to human form. The fire had thankfully warmed up the house enough to make quick work of chasing away the chill.

Ntare sat by the fireplace with another mug of tea in his hand. "Here's hoping the twins don't scare off my stonemason with their antics, well intended or not."

Sipping his tea, he watched the snow falling against the darkening sky. A contentment he hadn't felt in many a year settled over him. He wondered if his wandering feet had finally found a place to rest.

Maybe this could be home.

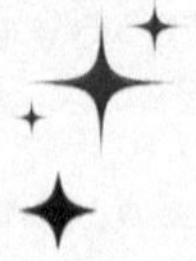

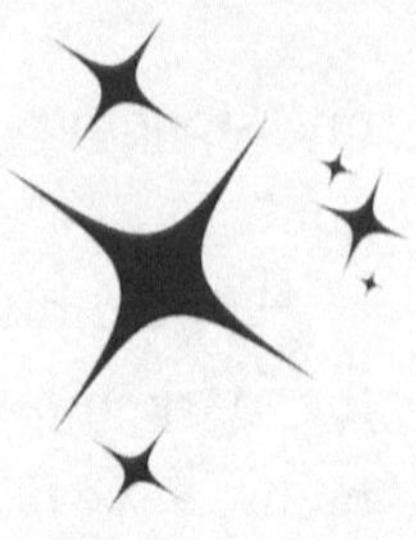

CHAPTER 5
WHEY

THE BANGING ON HIS DOOR WAS INCESSANT. WHEY groaned loudly when he heard Zuri shouting after another round of belligerent knocking. He dragged himself off the couch with enormous effort. The tincture had helped immensely, but he needed another twelve hours to be properly functional and not a stone zombie.

"You look like shite," Zuri said when he answered the door.

"Shite on a burned slice of toast, to be precise," Nsia agreed readily with her twin. "Feels wrong to start a row when you're like this."

"You're all heart." Whey tried to keep himself upright, but his strength was flagging. The twins lunged forward to grab him before he keeled over, dragging him back to the couch. "Had a flare-up."

"We can see that. Do you need the doctor? We can get Hamish or Wilfred… or take you to the clinic in South Myrddin." Nsia knelt by the couch. Her hand hovered above his forehead but didn't touch his skin. "You look absolutely done in. This why you left Ntare?"

"I had to get home before everything shut down on me." Whey closed his eyes, shifting onto his side further. "I gulped down my potion. Nothing else they can do for me. Just need rest. I'll apologise to him once I can stand up for longer than a few seconds. I didn't mean to be short with him."

"Are you sure we can't do anything?"

Whey cracked an eye open when a finger lightly ruffled his hair. "Never has been anything anyone could do. It is what it is. No more talking."

The twins watched him in silence for a few seconds. Whey closed his eyes, content to ignore them for the moment. A flurry of activity piqued his interest, and he couldn't resist looking, only to find Nsia and Zuri in the process of cleaning up his cottage.

They were a whirlwind of activity. It made him dizzy to watch, so he stopped trying to keep up. He fell asleep from one moment to the next, blissfully unaware of when they finished and left.

Whey awoke much later to a room bathed in the glowing light from the fireplace. The delicious scent of food wafted in from the kitchen. "Rocky? Have you been cooking?"

A happy squeak made him sit up slowly. He was grateful to find his body no longer felt weighed down by a load of granite. The ache had receded to a more manageable level.

Not gone.

It was never entirely gone.

He found Nsia in his kitchen with Rocky perched on her shoulder. "Have you been here all afternoon?"

"We left for a bit. Ntare insisted on sending over some of the stew he made. Something to warm you up." Nsia gestured to the large pot on the hob. "I'm heating it up for you. Rocky is, of course, playing supervisor."

Whey had known the Barbiers for as long as they'd been in South Myrddin. He'd done work on their fishery. Even in the face of his minor debacle with their friend, the kindness wasn't lost on him. "Thank you."

Nsia waved off his thanks. She ladled some of the stew into a bowl. "Let's get you back to the sofa so you can eat. Rocky's been taken care of. I made sure he's got fresh food and water. Fluffed up all his beds. How many of those does one hamster need?"

"Many." Whey allowed himself to be guided back to the couch. He chuckled at Rocky snuggled into Nsia's collar. "He'll be wanting to go home with you.

Abandoned by my furry friend. You didn't need to do all of this. I could manage."

"No one, not even a man made of stone, should be an island to themselves." Nsia placed the bowl of stew in his hands. "Ntare swears food has healing properties—and he's the expert. Eat up. I'll put Rocky back in his palace. You should rest up. Snow's falling thick and heavy now. I imagine you won't be able to get to his cottage for a few days."

"I'll apologise."

"A good start. And don't worry. We all know what it's like to have something out of our control impeding us. You're not the only person to struggle, Whey. Ntare has a lot of experience dealing with a chronic illness. He'll understand." Nsia gently lifted Rocky out of her collar and carried him over to the massive terrarium. "Do you need anything else?"

Whey shook his head. "It's manageable now—as much as it ever is. I promise I'll be fine. Thank you."

"There are enough leftovers for you to have stew for the next day or so. Make sure you put it away once it's cooled off some." Nsia hesitated for a few more seconds before finally saying her goodbyes. "I've stoked up your wood, so you should be fine to keep the fire going. Call Hamish or me if you need anything, all right? You have friends, Whey. Don't be afraid to give us a shout. And yes, I did let the druids know you weren't doing well."

"Shite. They'll hover. I'm fine." Whey ignored the knowing look she sent his way. "Okay, maybe not fine. I have a chronic illness. There's no permanent fix, so what options do I have?"

Silence followed. Nsia and her twin both suffered from a hereditary illness. One they never spoke about, though Whey knew it was the direct result of a curse placed on their family many centuries ago. They, more than many, understood the weight of what he faced.

Nsia eventually left him in peace. The stew had warmed him up. It might not be medicine, but he felt all the better for it.

Setting the bowl on the coffee table, Whey reclined back against the cushions. He'd always struggled with allowing himself to rest. He seemed to constantly find yet another task to accomplish until his body forced him to stop.

"You okay, Rocky?" Whey tilted his head to the side to glance at the terrarium, chuckling when a happy squeak sounded. "Good enough."

After a few minutes of watching the fire, Whey carried the empty bowl into the kitchen. He was surprised at the amount of food Ntare had sent over. A kind gesture, one that touched him. His abrupt exit had been rude at best, even if he'd had a justifiable reason.

Ntare had no reason to show kindness, yet he had. It made him appreciate his new client even more.

"We'll have to be on our best behaviour next time, won't we?" Whey plucked Rocky out of his burrow and held him gently. "I'll take him one of my tea blends as an apology and a thank-you. What do you think?"

Rocky squeaked before yawning and curling up in his hand.

"I'll take that as a yes."

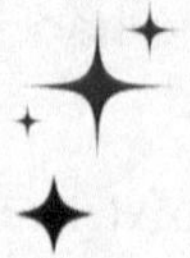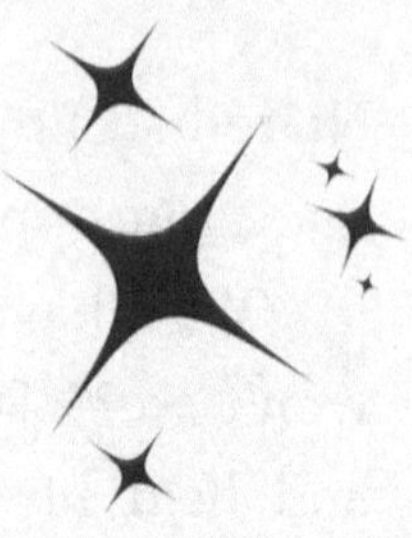

CHAPTER 6
NTARE

THE NOVELTY OF A FREEZING, FLUFFY WONDERLAND HAD yet to wear off. They'd quickly gone from a dusting to what felt like a blizzard. It had taken a couple of days before the sun melted away much of his icy playground.

His morning had started with a call from his contrite contractor. Whey had apologised, gruffly but earnestly, and promised to show up by nine. Ntare was excited to get the restoration back on track.

The apology had been appreciated but unnecessary. Ntare understood how a chronic illness could take the wind out of a person. He was impressed by Whey's self-awareness in knowing when rest was imperative; he had a terrible tendency to push beyond the point of exhaustion.

Stubbornness was one of his greatest strengths—and weaknesses.

Ntare puttered around the cottage with a large mug of tea in hand. It was too quiet without Fear and Wagu. Their chattering usually kept him company.

Here's hoping today goes better than the last time. One false start during the cottage restoration seemed more than sufficient.

Ntare took his mug of tea and stepped outside. He breathed in the crisp morning air and smiled.

It was beautiful, with the remnants of snow here and there. He had no regrets about finally putting roots down in one place. It had been time.

Ntare waved when a familiar van came up the narrow lane to park in front of the cottage. "Hello again."

Whey nodded. He moved around to the back of the van and began grabbing his tools. "Morning."

It was stilted. Awkward. Ntare hoped things settled down. Walking around on eggshells for the next few weeks would be a nightmare.

"Tea." Whey shoved a tin towards him. "For you. I make up the blends myself."

"Thank you."

The morning passed slowly. Ntare tried not to get in the way or intrude in his own home. It was difficult when all he heard was hammer against stone and the occasional grunt.

Ntare felt as though he were on the strangest and most prolonged first date in history. They danced around each other with furtive glances and half-started sentences. He wanted to laugh at the absurdity of it. Whey was his contractor. Nothing more, nothing less.

He poked his head into the kitchen after he couldn't take it any longer. "Would you care for some tea?"

Whey shot up. A cloud of dust flew up around him before settling onto his clothes and hair. His grumpy befuddlement was adorable in a way Ntare tried to ignore. "What?"

"Tea. Would you like some? I wanted to give the blend you brought a try." He was relieved when Whey nodded. "Brilliant."

Using an electric kettle in the living room, Ntare heated up water and brewed tea. He made up two mugs, carrying one into the kitchen. Whey accepted it with a grateful smile.

He sipped the tea for a second before setting the mug on a relatively empty spot on the counter. "I'm sorry…."

"One time, I called Zuri an ugly fish," Ntare blurted out. "My stomach had been in agony for days. She kept bugging me until I snapped. Think Nsia pissed herself laughing."

"Sounds like them." Whey brushed more of the stone dust from his shirt and hair. "I have a chronic pain disorder—one specific to my creature. I'm a gargoyle. Most days, it's bearable, but sometimes it flares up, and nothing helps. Not trying to excuse, just offer an explanation."

"At worst, you were a little brusque. It was confusing and mildly rude, not offensive or insulting. I understand. I accept your apology." Ntare didn't necessarily think what had happened was as bad as Whey had clearly built it up in his mind. He understood. Plenty of times, he'd felt he'd done something unforgivable, but it had been minor in reality. "Thank you for the tea… and the apology."

Whey lifted his mug in salute and had another sip. "I brought my favourite blend. Assam tea leaves that I mix with blood orange peels, rose hips, and hibiscus. Sweet, tangy, but strong. My preferred drink during the winter."

"The blood orange gives it the colour." Ntare could smell the fruitiness of the tea as he held the cup up close to his face. He took a tentative sip. "I can see why it's your favourite. This would pair beautifully with a spiced orange pastry I make. Once the kitchen is done, I'll bake some for you to try."

"That would be… nice." Whey set his mug down. He glanced around the kitchen and gestured to where all the stone had been removed. "It seems a disaster, but I promise it's actually better than it looks. The delicate part is done. Now, I can start with what I enjoy the most—building the walls back up. We've excised the nastiness like a bad tooth, and now I can fill in the gaps."

"Sounds painful."

"It is to the stone." Whey patted his hand on the wall. "It has a memory. All our memories and stories are retained within. The cottage is the body, but the stone is the skeleton. The mortar the veins. We breathe life into it."

"You speak about stone like I do food." Ntare saw his home but also Whey in a new light. "I'm glad the Barbiers didn't scare you off the job."

"They're not as terrifying as they think they are."

"Try telling them that."

"Not for a million pounds," Whey stated firmly. His lips twitched before he finally chuckled. "Maybe for two."

Ntare joined him in laughing. His gaze was drawn to how the smile deepened Whey's dimples and down to his lips for the briefest of moments. He cleared his throat and took a step back. "I should… I should let you get back to it. Can I make an early dinner for you? It's never fun to cook for just myself."

Whey held out his now-empty mug of tea. "After

having your stew, I'd be a fool to turn down another chance to try your cooking."

Ntare smiled again, feeling both pleased and a little embarrassed. "Thank you."

While Whey chiselled away at the stone, Ntare pondered over cooking options. He had plenty of experience using a fire when a kitchen wasn't available. There was a trivet and heavy-duty pan and pots specifically meant for using heat from the hearth. Maybe a steak and some kind of potatoes.

Simple, easy, yet delicious.

His lion had preened at Whey's praise. He had to resist the ridiculous urge to strut around proudly. They both clearly saw Whey as potential mate material, a rarity since his lion often railed against his dating choices. It manifested as a snarling inside him—an off-key note in a usually harmonious relationship between man and beast. Something as he'd gotten older, he'd started to pay more attention to.

I'm not asking Whey on a date.

He's my contractor.

A smug rumbling answered him in his mind. Ntare tried to refocus on what he'd need to do for dinner. A meal with Whey that was definitely not a date.

He ignored the tiny part of him that whispered, *But it could be.*

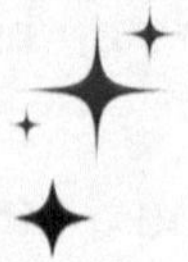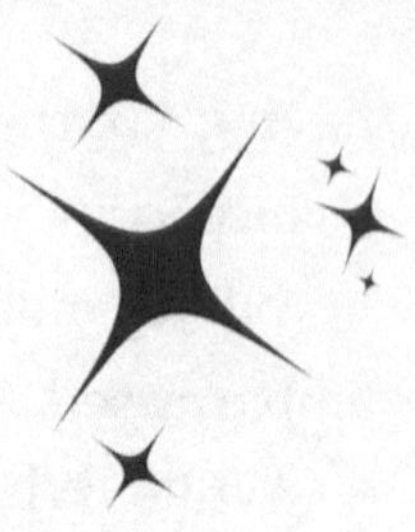

CHAPTER 7
WHEY

THE DAY HAD BEEN SUCCESSFUL. WHEY HAD MADE GOOD progress on the kitchen walls. It helped that the space was small, and his natural affinity for stone also sped things up.

A regular mason might take three to four days on a job that Whey would complete in one. He would be done with the kitchen tomorrow and be able to move on to the next section. He pressed the palm of his hand against the wall. The stone hummed happily against his skin.

Each restoration job was different. Some homes retained the happiness and joy of their previous owners; others had soaked in the anger and strife. This cottage held comfort deep within its veins.

Once Whey had cleaned up for the day, he ensured his tools and equipment wouldn't be in the way if

Ntare had to be in the kitchen. Since he'd be on the job for the next few weeks, he didn't see a point in repeatedly packing everything up, only to bring it out the following morning. He washed his hands and dusted off his clothes.

The rich scent of herbs, spices, and butter drew him into the living room. Whey watched in fascination as Ntare weaved his unique brand of magic. For some, he knew cooking was more than a necessity. It was an art.

Though Whey would never admit it out loud, he'd been more distracted than on any other job. Something about Ntare kept grabbing his attention. It wasn't simply surface attraction. Though Ntare was incredibly handsome, it felt far deeper than that.

In no time at all, Ntare handed over a generous portion of roasted potatoes, steak, and pan-fried flatbread. A simple meal, though spiced and seasoned to perfection. His mouth was alive with flavours he didn't recognise but instantly adored.

It wasn't a date. Whey told himself that repeatedly, even though it felt like one. They were sharing a meal and some homemade wine, just a small glass that went well with the steak.

It wasn't a date.

It wasn't.

Whey relaxed into the comfortable armchair. His legs stretched out in front of him with the plate balanced on his thigh. "Thanks for this. I haven't had a meal this good in ages. You've got a gift."

"'An affinity for the delectable' is what an old friend used to call it." Ntare took both plates, carried them into the kitchen, and then returned with a bottle. "More wine?"

"Maybe next time?" Whey stared down at the empty glass in his hand. He didn't want to make any assumptions, but the meal was fraught with tension and fervent looks. They'd both been ridiculous in their attempts to subtly observe each other. "Will there be one?"

"I...." Ntare poured himself more wine, taking a sip and seeming embarrassed when some spilt over the rim as his fingers trembled. "I'd like there to be one."

Whey placed his cup on the coffee table and stood up. He stepped closer to Ntare, gently plucking the glass out of his hand to avoid more wine spilling. "I don't usually.... I always seem to work for little old crones or mangy wolves. Mild exaggeration. I should have a policy about not dating clients. Probably bad for business."

"Probably."

Whey stood far closer to Ntare than was good for his senses. He was drawn in deeper by the myriad of emotions on his face, a reflection of his own conflicted thoughts. The beginnings of attraction warred with cautious uncertainty. "I'd like to do this again."

"A meal?

"A meal. Some wine. A hint of more to come. Maybe even a kiss goodbye?" Whey knew it was too soon, but something drew him to Ntare. A feeling he hadn't had before. It made him want to take the risk. "An official date. Not just food and us pretending we're not staring at each other the entire time."

"You feel it too?" Ntare placed a hand on his own chest above his heart, then reached out with his other to rest on Whey's in the same spot. "The connection? The beginnings of one. My lion says… mate, though I've never known any shifter to experience something like this."

"Gargoyles do. Or at least, according to family lore. We have a history of fate intervening in annoying and inopportune moments." Whey brought his hand up to cover Ntare's. "I don't have anyone I can ask from the Southcott side. I can delve into the few books and journals; maybe Hyde can hunt something down for me. They're a wizard when it comes to finding the most obscure texts."

"Could we actually be mates in the soulmate sense?" Ntare sounded almost awed by the idea.

"How about we stick with a first date? An official one. We'll let whatever cosmic mischief wants to play with us alone." Whey tried for confident, though the way Ntare's heartbeat vibrated through him made him think it was a pointless endeavour to imagine they could avoid fate. "Maybe we can lay the foundation for more than your cottage."

He smiled at Whey, nodding after a moment. "I'd like that."

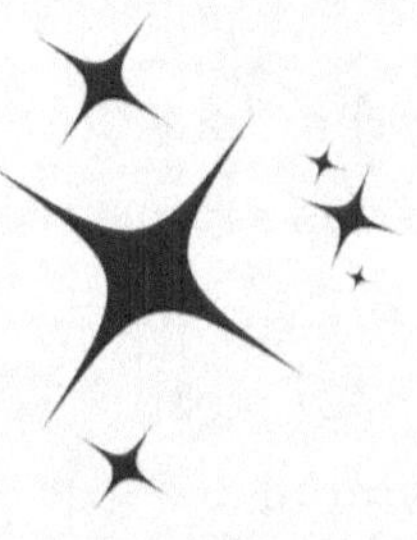

CHAPTER 8
NTARE

THE COTTAGE SEEMED HOLLOW AND VAST WITHOUT HIS feathered friends and Whey to keep him company. Ntare lay in bed for hours without being able to sleep. His mind refused to stop racing.

Stripped down to his boxers and without a blanket, Ntare still felt the heat and weight of Whey's hand on his skin. Their combined heartbeats echoed in his ears. He ran his fingers over his chest, feeling the lingering ghost of his touch.

Fated mates.

Soulmates.

Many scoffed at the concept. Ntare had never been enough of a romantic to be sold on the idea of someone being meant for him. Soulmates were rare enough to be the relationship version of a unicorn.

But now, part of him wondered if Whey had been

what had drawn him to Scotland when he'd initially been against the idea.

Ntare rolled out of bed, hissing at the cold stone underneath his bare feet. He cursed the weather and impulsive moving decisions.

There had been nothing more enjoyable than walking barefoot across warm sands or through soft grass. Icy cold stone didn't hold quite the same appeal. He was definitely going to need slippers.

Warm, furry ones.

Ntare grumbled his way into the en suite, turning on the tap and waiting impatiently for it to heat up. He splashed hot water on his face and tried to chase away sleep. "Carpets. Lots of them. All over. Why is it so cold? It's unnatural."

Still whingeing under his breath, Ntare stalked towards the living room. He stoked the fire, feeling as if he was slowly thawing from a deep freeze. Maybe a mild exaggeration. Movement at the window caught his attention.

"Well, no wonder." Ntare stared out at the thick blanket of snow once again covering everything in sight. He shivered when a blast of wind buffeted the cottage. "I wonder if Whey is all right." The last winter storm had been brutal on him.

Ntare fussed about for a while, making breakfast and pointedly avoiding his phone. He tried to casually sip his herbal tea. Still, his mind kept coming up with increasingly dramatic scenarios about what might be happening to Whey.

Was he okay? Would the weather bother him as it had a few days earlier? Should he call or wait, or could he drive over to check on him?

Ten minutes passed in what felt like hours. He kept reaching for his phone and then stopping himself.

The logical thing would be to call him. It was well past the time Whey had intended to start for the day. Ntare had a perfectly valid reason for giving him a ring.

And he had tried in his mind, at least, to make the call, imagining the conversation. He loathed talking on the phone. It always felt like a massive bother.

I'll text him.

There was, of course, no response to his message. Ntare couldn't shake the nagging feeling that something was wrong. What if Whey couldn't call for help or reach his mobile?

His lion roared in his chest, wanting them to check on their mate. It was ridiculous. They barely knew him at all at this point.

Yet Ntare found himself heading out into a winter storm to check on Whey. Nothing impulsive or foolish about an attempt to drive in the snow. At least, that was what he kept telling himself as his vehicle fishtailed on the snow and ice-covered roads. He had no doubts this was a fool's errand.

"I am an absolute knobhead. What am I doing?" Ntare cursed loudly when he suddenly lost control of the vehicle and skidded violently off the road into a hedge. He cut the engine after several futile attempts to reverse. "Well, brilliant. I am well and truly stuck in the middle of the snowstorm."

He rubbed his hand across his chest to ease the tension. Ntare and his lion were rarely at odds. There was no point. It would be warring within himself, which had always seemed counterintuitive.

It would be wiser to stay with his vehicle. His lion disagreed. Their mate might be in trouble, but that was all that mattered to its mind.

"We *are* in trouble." Ntare tried to reason with his shifter half while leaning against the vehicle. He had been unable to budge it no matter what he tried. *And you don't care. You want to hunt out Whey.*

The urge to shift became unbearable. Ntare surrendered to his lion. He stalked around his wrecked vehicle in seconds, leaving massive pawprints in the snow.

His lion immediately sensed Whey. He abandoned the vehicle, using it to help leap over the hedge and head across a snowy field. They were, it seemed, going on an adventure—a cold adventure.

If nothing else, Ntare was grateful for the added protection of his thick coat of fur. The cold didn't penetrate quite the way it had in his human form. He wondered what Whey was going to say when a massive lion scratched at his front door.

Lions weren't native to Scotland, but Ntare was pleased to live in a world where shifters were common. No one looked twice at a random animal prancing through the forest. Though he imagined some of the farmers might not be pleased if he frightened the sheep half to death.

After skirting the inlet, Ntare headed through a thicket of trees and wound up on a lane. He knew instinctively they were close. It wasn't a surprise when, at the end of the road, he spotted a familiar van sitting in front of a cottage.

Ntare shifted back to himself, grateful his clothes stayed on him through the change. It would've been mortifying to pop up starkers in front of Whey's home. He raised his hand to knock on the door, only for it to open before he could. "Morning?"

"I got a call warning me about a lion seen prowling around." Whey's grey eyes sparkled with amusement. "Know anything about it?"

"Trying to keep warm?" Ntare shivered when a powerful blast of wind went right through him. "Fur helps."

"What are you doing out in this weather? I was going to call you to cancel, but my phone's dead at the moment. It's charging now." Whey caught him by the arm, dragging him inside the cottage. "I'll make you some tea. Have you eaten? Why didn't you call?"

"I… tried texting once but didn't want to be pushy or seem odd. But then I couldn't help thinking you might be in trouble and couldn't reach your phone." Ntare cringed while continuing to brush snow off himself. "So, I stalked you in person instead?"

Whey stared at him silently for several long seconds before his shoulders shook as he burst out laughing. "Where's your car?"

"Stuck in a ditch somewhere." Ntare sighed when Whey laughed even harder. He couldn't help chuckling himself. "I was worried something had happened to you because the weather was so cold."

"That's very kind of you. I'm amazed you even made it halfway. Roads aren't always passable when the weather turns, particularly during a snowstorm." Whey shuffled around in his kitchen woodenly. His movements were careful and measured. "I planned to call you once my phone got enough charge to be turned on. It's being recalcitrant this morning for reasons I cannot explain. Though I think my body feels the same."

"Next time I buy a remote cottage, I'll plan the

restorations for a warmer time of year." He wandered over to inspect the terrarium off the kitchen. A tiny hamster poked its head out before ducking out of sight. "Or buy an island somewhere in the Caribbean with all the money I don't have."

"You could plan your move in the summer next time," Whey teased. "Have you eaten? I was getting around to having tea and maybe some leftovers. There's more than enough for two."

"My lion wanted to find you." Ntare ignored the question and blurted out the first thing on his mind. He groaned internally, keeping his face pointed towards the terrarium. "Not that I didn't want to check on you. I did."

Truth be told, his lion had never been happier. A new home, new territory, and the beginning of a relationship with his mate. Ntare had honestly found it hard to settle down; it had aggravated his stomach enough for him to have a double dose of his medicinal tea.

"The only mated couples I'm aware of outside of my family are shifters. I imagine your lion knew before either of us did." Whey dragged his fingers through his silver hair, turning to lean against the counter. "I'm a dab hand at tuning out my gargoyle. The shift inflames my condition, possibly causing it to progress. I've had to learn how to ignore it."

Ntare's heart broke at the pain in Whey's voice. He couldn't imagine being separated from a part of himself. "Does it tear you apart?"

"Not anymore. I don't have a choice. The pain is so debilitating—worse if I shift. The chronic illness is what one might call the fracture in my stone." Whey shook his head after a moment of contemplative silence, seeming to push away his sadness. "Let me put the kettle on for tea."

Ntare reached out after the briefest hesitation and wrapped his arms around Whey. He tensed before relaxing into the embrace. "I'm so sorry. For the physical pain and the emotional torment of being forced to cut off part of yourself."

Whey slowly wound his arms around Ntare. He held on tightly to him, taking a deep breath before pulling away. He cleared his throat and blinked rapidly for a second. "Thank you."

Ntare managed a smile through the overwhelming tide of emotion washing over him. The short embrace had sealed the connection between them. "What are mates for?"

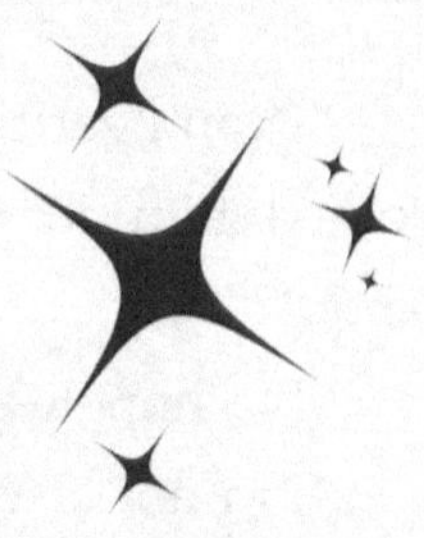

CHAPTER 9
WHEY

THE WHISTLING KETTLE BROKE THROUGH THE PROLONGED silence. Whey moved mechanically, processing things slowly. His nan had always said he inherited it from his granddad. He could hear her muttering, "Smart as a whip, but slow to change, like a volcano creating an island."

Or like moving granite up a mountain.

While Whey dithered over tea, Ntare had communed with Rocky. His hamster was, as always, thrilled by any attention given to him. He smiled at the conversation happening between the two—one-sided but sweet nonetheless.

Part of him wanted to flee from what seemed like an immense amount of pressure. Two things stopped him: the weather and the hope of something special. He was also unlikely to outrun a lion.

"I can hear the rocks grinding in your head." Ntare joined him in the kitchen. "What are you thinking about?"

"I'm hopeless at relationships."

"I'm not a whiz at them either." He leaned against one of the counters. "Maybe fate decided we needed all the help we could get? A nudge in the right direction?"

Whey finished procrastinating with the tea, handing one of the mugs to Ntare. Their fingers touched, sending a jolt of electric energy surging through him. "I've had the same question going through my mind since yesterday. Do we run with it or from it?"

"What do you want to do?" Ntare took a sip of the tea, wincing at the heat and setting it on the counter to cool.

"Running is so very undignified." Whey snickered when Ntare laughed. "At least, that's what my nan would've said."

"Would she?"

"Nan Southcott believed in soulmates." Whey nodded to a dainty leather notebook that he'd left on his small kitchen table. "Dug that out of a box last night. She didn't meet hers, but her mother did, and so did her brother. They've all passed away. I've a cousin who lives halfway around the world, I think. I haven't heard from them in ages. I've no one to ask, but she wrote quite a bit about it in her journal."

"Oh? Find anything of interest?"

"If you ever want to traumatise yourself, read through your nan's diary from her twenties and thirties. She was quite… descriptive." Whey shuddered. He rolled his eyes when Ntare laughed for a second time. "In any case, she mentioned the instant connection. The… jolt of energy, or kinetic emotion as she called it, that transferred from one to the other upon touching."

Ntare reached out to the journal. "May I?"

Whey simply nodded. He went over to dig around in the refrigerator for the leftovers. "I'll heat these up for us. We can eat and pore over my nan's romantic ramblings."

"I don't want to run away from it."

Whey glanced back over his shoulder to find Ntare holding the journal in his hands. "Neither do I."

"Did this provide any insights into what to expect? Aside from the jolt of energy?" Ntare had yet to open the journal.

"You can read for yourself. She wouldn't mind." Whey paused for a moment while continuing to inspect the contents of the fridge. "If I'm honest, she'd probably encourage it."

"Oh?"

"Nan always hoped I'd find someone." Whey turned back to the fridge. He finally found the leftovers, grabbed them, and shut the door. "Let me heat this up."

Setting the pot of stew on the hob, Whey allowed himself a moment to think. Ntare's presence had forced him to face facts head-on. He had a mate; a bond had formed between them.

They'd tried to be calm and casual about it. It was clear to him they were both repressing the urge to confront the situation. They were both afraid of being vulnerable when it had barely even been a matter of days or hours.

In past relationships, Whey had often been accused of being emotionally unavailable. He'd been told his heart was made of stone. It had never been his intention to keep everything so close to the vest, but he hoarded the deeper parts of himself like a dragon in its lair.

Maybe this time, he could be different.

Whey rested his hand on the wall next to the stove. It always grounded him to touch his fingers to rough-hewn stone. The closest to shifting into his gargoyle that he could get. He inhaled slowly, calming his nerves and heart down. *I can do this.*

"Holding the wall up?"

"Who better than a gargoyle?" Whey returned his

attention to the stew, giving it a stir. He realised they had a chance at something special if he wanted to try—and he did. "I think this could be the start...."

"Of lunch?" Ntare remarked when the silence became strained. He was kindly giving Whey an out if he wanted it. "An early one."

"Relationships are like one of my restoration projects. It takes a strong bond. There's no perfect wall. Lines are crooked, stones rough. When put together right, not even the harshest gale can shake its foundation." Whey scratched his head for a second. "Metaphor may have lost the plot somewhere in the middle. Or maybe I did."

"Are you saying I'm built like a stone cottage? I don't remember the song going that way." Ntare smiled when Whey chuckled. "I'm deflecting."

"A trait we share. Though you do it with far better humour than I ever have." Whey turned the heat down, allowing the stew to simmer for a few more minutes. "I don't want to be a man made of stone when it comes to relationships anymore. And yes, I'm aware it's ironic, given I'm a gargoyle."

Ntare closed the distance between them, taking the spoon from him and balancing it on the pot. His fingers slotted between Whey's perfectly, and he enjoyed the slight jolt of energy flitting across his skin at the contact. "I've spent my life travelling, always afraid to stay too long in one place. Ever the lone lion without a pride."

"And now?" Whey held his breath. He tried not to think about how perfectly their hands fit together. Both calloused and strong, as if they were made for each other.

"Now I think maybe I've found the solid rock that I was searching for."

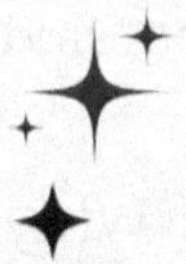

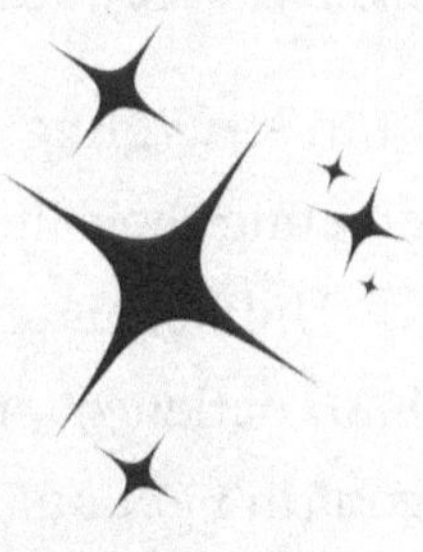

CHAPTER 10
NTARE
ONE YEAR LATER

Ntare woke with a start to a quiet snuffling by his ear. He plucked Rocky off his pillow and set him on his chest. "You have an escaped rodent."

"You're his favourite." Whey took a squeaking Rocky and returned him to one of his many homes within the cottage. "I have tea brewing, but I've left the brekkie for you."

A year had flown by. The stone restoration had been completed months ago. Whey had stuck around to help with the rest of the renovations on the cottage. They'd spent so much time together over the course of the last twelve months. Ntare had worried the close quarters might begin to grate on them. It hadn't.

If anything, each day had strengthened their bond. Ntare had developed a deep love for the taciturn gargoyle. They were uniquely suited for each other, both struggling with their own chronic conditions and creating their life within them.

Unlike his experience in past relationships, Whey had patience on the hard days, the ones where he couldn't get out of bed or where he seemed to maintain permanent residence in the loo. It was a relief to be with a man who understood. Someone who had been in his shoes or a variation of them.

It was a relief to be bluntly truthful and open on those days. They picked each other up when they fell. Sometimes, they simply sat and allowed the other to rant about the wrongness of it all.

Whey understood when Ntare grumbled about the pointlessness of suffering. He didn't fumble around with wasted platitudes. There didn't have to be a lesson in the pain or something good coming from it.

It just… was. And that was okay. Maybe not *okay*, but it simply was.

"Whisker for your thoughts?"

Ntare rolled his eyes at him. "Only if I get a rock for yours."

"Stomach bothering you?" Whey sat on the edge of the bed. He gently ran his hand along Ntare's side, carefully avoiding applying any pressure. "Want some of the herbal tea that Emrys recommended? It seemed to help last time."

"No." Ntare captured Whey's hand, using it to pull

himself up into a seated position, bringing them closer. "It's not my stomach."

"You sure?"

He brought his other hand up, running his fingers along Whey's face. He traced the sharp lines of his jaw. "I'm sure. How about I make something special for breakfast?"

"Everything you make is special. You're a wizard in the kitchen."

"And a lion in the sheets?" Ntare was serious for a moment before they both burst out laughing. He rested the palm of his hand on the side of Whey's face once they'd settled down. "I love you."

Whey's smile widened. He turned his head to brush a kiss against Ntare's hand. "My feelings for you are etched in stone."

"Hands down, the cheesiest thing you've said to date."

"I'll have to try harder." Whey leaned in for a kiss.

Behind closed doors, Ntare had found Whey had a silly side that he didn't often show. Something he'd never expected from the stone-faced gargoyle. He adored being privy to that part of him.

Being trusted with the softer side… the vulnerable aspects of him.

Whey always talked about building a solid foundation. Ntare didn't know if it was the gargoyle in him or the stonemason, maybe a combination of both. But he had a point. Relationships even between bonded mates required one.

"Another winter storm is rolling in—or floating in." Whey got up from the bed, wandering over to peer out the window. "I've already cancelled my job at Ada's orchard. The fix to her farmhouse will have to wait. Snow's already falling thick and fast. I'm not anxious to aggravate the aches and pains by trying to redo stone walls in the middle of snow and ice. Just my bad luck."

"I disagree." Ntare sat up, pushing the blankets away and rubbing the sleep from his eyes. He yawned wildly while stretching languidly. "It's been good luck for us."

"How do you figure?"

"The last winter storm brought you to my door… then me to yours." Ntare stalked over to join Whey by the window, slipping his arm around the gargoyle's waist and leaning in to drop a kiss against his neck. "And that was the very best luck I've ever had in my entire life."

The End

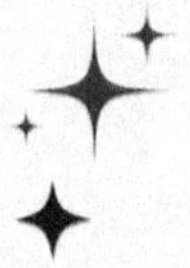
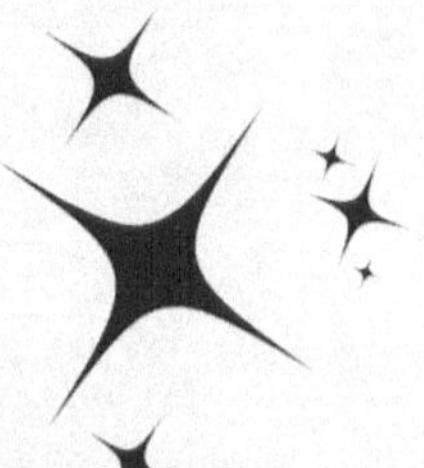

PAY THE PIPER

Two beautiful shifters have one amazingly satisfying night. Aroha Kiri spends most of her time making beautiful jewellery. She finds herself delightfully distracted by a roaming bagpipe-playing dancer who moves to the beat of her own rhythm.

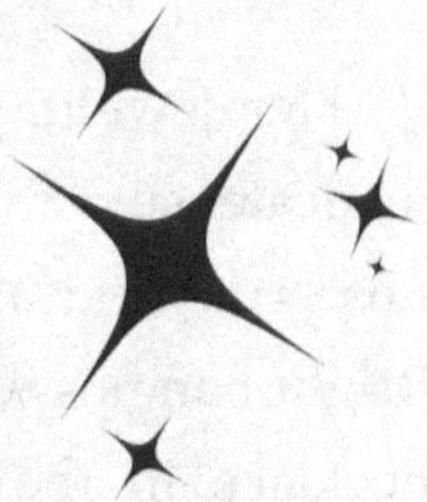

AROHA

The haunting melody caught Aroha's attention almost immediately. It resonated within her bones and brought an immediate question to her mind. Who in the name of the goddess was playing bagpipes at eight in the morning?

It took her a moment to recognise the tune, a slightly Hindi take on "Loch Lomond," a folk song often sung in the pub on an evening out. Aroha set down her tools and pulled the magnifying lenses off her head. She stepped out of her shop to find the source of the music.

The Jain twins followed a woman who could only be their cousin. The bagpiper had long, flowing brown hair and eyes almost as dark as her own. She wore a short tartan dress with a black corset and a long lace cloak.

Her jewellery caught Aroha's eyes. All beautiful, intricate silver. The delicate chain strung between a nose ring and an earring glinted in the morning sun. Bright bangles were stacked along her wrists. A corded necklace in the shape of a sinewy serpent dangled down, disappearing between the beautiful swell of the top of her breasts.

There was something in the sway of her hips. The jolly yet haunting tune pulled from the bagpipes. Aroha almost wanted to trail after her like the woman was the Pied Piper, following wherever the path might lead.

She danced along the lane, pausing to greet Aroha. "Morning."

With a wicked smirk and a wink, the bagpiper bowed slightly before lifting her head. Aroha could only watch, mesmerised, as she danced off with her music trailing behind her. She barely managed to stop herself from following after her.

"Meet our cousin, Pari Jain or PJ." Constable Vidya Jain joined Aroha where she still stood. "Bram convinced her to treat the village to an early-morning serenade. "She's visiting from Edinburgh. She left the family when we did but wanted a larger city to settle in and find her way."

"Quite the set of pipes." Aroha nodded towards the

beautiful bagpipes that had an intricately carved snake curving around them. "Never seen one like it."

"Vain thing that she is. The snake is designed to look like PJ in her snake form. She's a shifter." Vidya shook her head and chuckled. "I better follow her before she gets herself in trouble. If you want to hear more, she promised Bram she would join him at the pub this evening for a music session."

"I always enjoy an evening at the pub."

"Tea?" Rosa had come out from her bakery, holding a mug towards Aroha. They'd been good friends for years. "Have you seen her, then?"

"Heard her first—as is usually the case with our cousin." Trishna stood beside her twin. Both were out of their usual police uniform. "She's only here for a few days before her wandering feet carry her off to another village to torture with the caterwauling."

"She's beautiful. I mean, the music is beautiful." Aroha cleared her throat, ignoring the amused looks sent by the twins especially.

As they watched, PJ veered off the lane towards Raven Park and the loch in the distance. Aroha sipped her tea, unable to tear her gaze away from the dancing figure. She truly was the most striking woman she'd ever seen.

"She's a whirling dervish—a force of nature." Trishna

remained by Aroha while her twin waved goodbye and then wandered off after PJ. "She's left more than one broken heart behind when they had expectations. Not her fault when she's bluntly truthful about her preferences."

"Is she?"

"'Forewarned is forearmed.' Isn't that the phrase, adage, or whatever people call it?" Trishna gave her arm a gentle pat. "She's never cruel and always honest. Other people's expectations aren't her responsibility."

"Are you trying to write her dating profile? It needs some work." Aroha sipped her tea. She watched the dancing figure in the distance, appreciating the music and curves. "This is the most Scottish morning I've ever had in the village."

Trishna shook her head with an almost hysterical laugh. "She certainly doesn't need my help. You just had a familiar glint in your eyes—and I didn't want to be arresting her for breaking another heart."

"Not sure that's a crime. If it eases your worries, I prefer fun, brief connections to prolonged relationships." Aroha had never been one to fall in love or need a deeper romantic connection. She liked the company of others—and Pari Jain was just the type of woman she wanted to enjoy. "Introduce us?"

Trishna eyed her for a second before finally nodding. "You two are going to be trouble—I can just tell."

"I am never trouble."

"Sure. Now, I better follow those two to ensure they don't wind up in the loch or something else ridiculous." Trishna said her goodbyes to Aroha and Rosa, walking down the lane towards the park. "We'll be at the pub tonight. I'll introduce you."

They watched in silence for a few minutes. Aroha still wanted to follow, but the siren call of an unfinished necklace kept her standing on the pavement. Rosa stayed with her, sipping tea and watching the three figures until they disappeared.

"The thing I have always appreciated about South Myrddin is how we never have to explain ourselves. No one cares or judges. They expect we know our own minds—thoughts, dreams, and feelings." Rosa said almost precisely what Aroha had been thinking. "Maybe it's what draws all of us here and keeps us from moving on. The open and ready acceptance."

"You're not wrong." Aroha had another sip of her tea. "Thanks for this. Good blend."

"I had a delivery yesterday. I haven't come up with a name for it yet. Sweet and floral with a bit of a spice kick." Rosa lifted her cup and sniffed it. "Smells divine. The entire bakery is filled with it since I opened the box and brewed a batch."

"How about the Pied Piper?" Aroha grinned when

Rosa sent her a knowing look. "Sweet, floral, and spicy?"

"You're incorrigible. Fine. The Pied Piper tea blend it is. I'm sure it'll go down a treat." Rosa patted her on the shoulder. "I best get back to the bakery. I've got pastries in the oven. Want me to save you one?"

"Always." She thought, perhaps, another benefit of their village was the fantastic food. From fresh baked goods to Italian-Cajun fusion to Wok Away, there was almost everything one could wish for in South Myrddin, surprising given how small it was. It was a testament to the eclectic group of beings who called it home. "Save me a couple. I'll share with Hyde since I have a book to pick up later."

"Fair enough. You've got about thirty minutes."

"Perfect. Just enough time to finish the necklace." Aroha waved at Rosa, who shadowed back to her bakery instead of walking. "Lazy vampire."

Chuckling to herself, Aroha walked back into Unclouded Light, her beloved jewellery shop that she'd named after a Robert Burns poem. Like many of the places in the village, she had an apartment above the business on the ground floor. It made the morning journey to work incredibly easy.

Once sat at her workspace, Aroha placed the magnifying lenses back on her head, drawing them down to cover her eyes. It allowed her to get up close and personal with the necklace. She grabbed one of her carving tools, a set made by a fae blacksmith specifically for the purpose of allowing her to design straight onto metal, be it silver or gold.

Her original intentions had been to design an Imbolc theme. The necklace was a series of connected silver discs. As she touched the tool to the first one, her vision changed on her. She lost herself to the creation of a slithering and seductive serpent winding its way along the piece.

Unclouded Light had been something of a dream come true for her. Aroha Kiri had taken both of her names from her maternal grandmother, a Māori healer and panther shifter. She had inherited the latter part from her mother.

When her grandmother and mother died, Aroha was left the sole panther shifter in a family who didn't understand her. She'd been ostracised as a result. Perhaps she'd been a painful reminder of the lineage that had been lost; she'd never fully understood it.

With a broken and grieving spirit, Aroha had left her home and travelled the world. She'd met a pair of fox shifters, the Thams, who'd suggested Scotland. She'd come to South Myrddin with no expectations and found herself welcomed with open arms.

She had managed to build a successful business in the village. However, there were times when she travelled to markets outside Scotland. The brief trips soothed the part of her that craved adventure and longed for the home of her maternal ancestors.

Pushing her wandering thoughts out of her mind, Aroha returned to the necklace. She had finished the basic design of the serpent. Now, she began adding the tiniest of melanite stones. They fit perfectly into her creation, adding a shine to scales and reminding her of glittering dark eyes that had promised all sorts of mischief.

Aroha finally set down her tools. She stretched her arms above her head, her long sleeves falling to reveal the lines of tattoos covering her skin, all in homage to her grandmother.

Rest here, little serpent. Perhaps I'll find a home for you later.

A quick glance at her watch showed she'd worked far longer than intended. The sun was already setting. Her stomach made its presence known, grumbling at her having worked through lunch. Something she had a bad habit of doing when a design grabbed her attention and demanded to be finished.

Taking a couple of biscuits to tide her over for the moment, Aroha had a quick shower to wash away the day. She found herself eagerly anticipating an evening at the pub. There would be food and music, dancing and laughter. There would also be a beautiful, enchanting serpent there to tempt her.

Aroha had supped and drunk at The Spiked Cauldron a thousand times. She'd never been overly bothered about her attire. One night, she'd even gone in grubby overalls with her magnifying lenses still resting on her head. *What am I doing?*

The majority of her clothing had been bought with utility and comfort in mind. Did it keep her warm? Was it going to get caught on anything in the shop? Would it bother her if she accidentally burned a hole in it?

Those were the questions she kept in mind while shopping. There was, however, one section of her closet dedicated to the sole purpose of showing off her jewellery. Her collection was massive—partly her creations, along with vintage pieces bought on her travels around the world.

As a panther shifter, Aroha tended to run warmer than others, but even so, the Scottish winters could be brutal. She grabbed a black turtleneck and tight jeans that fit her like a glove. She spent longer on selecting her jewellery than the clothing.

Once adorned with sufficient sparkling wonder, Aroha left the shop and stepped into the crisp evening air. She waved at Teresa and Hyde, who were walking down the lane towards the pub. Much of the village appeared to be answering the siren call of the visiting bagpiper.

"Evening, you two." Aroha crossed over the lane to join the couple. She admired Hyde's vintage blazer. "I've a new pin that would go beautifully with the deep burgundy of that."

"Oh. Shiny things?" Hyde perked up immediately. They pointed to the They and Hello pins on the collar of their blazer. "Would it go with these?"

"This one has cats. It's not an exact match to your chaos gremlins, but it's probably fifty years old. A fellow jeweller sent it to me from somewhere in southern France. I'd mentioned wanting to find something feline." Aroha had grown to adore Hyde, like much of the village did. The quiet and quirky bookshop owner who was always willing to hunt down a book, no matter how rare, if you asked them. "How about I bring it around tomorrow?"

"Brilliant. Mortar and Pestle will highly approve—vain things that they are." Hyde fell silent for a while. They had their arm looped through Teresa's. The two made a sweet couple. "Did you see PJ the bagpiper?"

"Saw and heard." Aroha toyed with the long chain around her neck. "She's… charming."

Teresa raised an eyebrow, grinning knowingly at her while Hyde simply kept walking. "Caught your eye, did she?"

"I think Pari Jain, the bagpiper, would catch even the eye of one of the scarecrows in Ada's orchard." Aroha refused to acknowledge the still-grinning Teresa. "It promises to be a fun night at the pub."

"It's *almost* always a fun night at The Spiked Cauldron." Hyde reached up to adjust their cap before glancing between Teresa and Aroha. "Have I missed something?"

"I'm teasing Aroha." Teresa winked at her and then turned to Hyde. "I think she's more than noticed our wandering piper."

"Noticed her as what?" Hyde wanted to know. They paused to wave at Bram across the lane, who was also heading towards the pub with his guitar across his back. "What did she notice her as?"

"A beautiful woman with a seductive sway to her hips." Teresa continued on when Hyde just frowned at her. "Aroha finds her attractive."

"Ah. Oh." Hyde's eyes went wide, and they glanced towards Aroha. "Really? You'll like PJ. She's fun. Not like that. I don't know her in that way."

Aroha had to chuckle at the sudden rambling from Hyde. "I know what you meant."

"Good." Hyde fell silent as the pub came into view.

A night at The Spiked Cauldron could be raucous or calm. Tonight was likely to be of the former. She heard the music long before they arrived at the pub.

Hyde reached into their pocket to retrieve ear protectors, pulling them over their head. "It's going to be a loud night."

The three made their way inside the pub. Bram had arrived before them. He had already brought a chair to sit near PJ and was preparing his guitar. Other village musicians joined in with them, adding a fiddle and a tin whistle, followed shortly by a bodhran, which added a lovely rhythm to everything.

It was no surprise when Teresa made her way over. Her voice had a magic all its own. Aroha knew she wasn't the only one to be carried away by it.

Moving through the pub, Aroha ordered herself a pint of ale. A new one from a Highlands brewery. She sipped her drink at the bar before moving to find a seat. She ignored Teresa's knowing grin when she sat close to the lovely bagpiper.

Enchanting. Entrancing. Enticing.

There were probably other words to describe Pari Jain—better ones. All were correct. Aroha hadn't been able to tear her gaze away from the bagpiper.

Those glittering brown eyes glanced her way repeatedly. PJ danced and played, weaving her way through the crowd. She passed Aroha several times, lingering, then moving only to return as if drawn to her.

For those moments, everyone faded away. All that

remained was the music and the two of them. Each glance became heated. Every sway of her hips seemed an invitation.

After an hour, Aroha retreated to a quiet corner of the pub. She noshed on a particularly large bridie and sipped from her second pint of ale. The flaky pastry was filled with a delicious meat and onion mixture. Her overactive shifter metabolism made it harder for her to get properly drunk. Also, it meant she ate more throughout the day.

The warmth of the pub washed over her. It came from both the fireplace and the community within. Like much of the village, it offered a soothing balm on a rough day.

"Hello again."

"He—" Aroha tried not to choke to death on the last crumb of pastry she'd inhaled. She had never in her life felt so clumsy and undignified. Clearing her throat, she made a second attempt. "Hello."

"Pari Jain. Most everyone calls me PJ." She nodded to the empty seat at the small table. "Can I join you?"

"Of course." Aroha tried to subtly brush the dusting of pastry flakes from the table and her shirt. Her jewellery jangled noisily to her sensitive hearing, making her attempts futile. She sighed to herself and instead focused on the beautiful woman across from her. "Fancy a pint? The ale varies from decent to extraordinary, depending on how many you've had."

"Well, how could I possibly turn one down? Especially from you." PJ's brown eyes once again glinted with mischief and promise. It was intoxicating, simply staring into them—almost hypnotic. "I haven't seen you before on my brief visits to this part of the world."

"I travel a few times a year, hunting for raw materials and vintage pieces for my shop." Aroha reached up to touch one of the necklaces around her neck. "I found this one last August in a little seaside village halfway around the world."

"Did you?" PJ leaned across the table, reaching out to pick up the pendant and inspect it. It brought them just a hair's breadth apart. "It's beautiful. Want to go for a walk?"

"A walk?" Aroha glanced towards the musicians' corner of the room, where things seemed to be picking up again. It gave her a moment's grace from the intensity of the woman inches from her. "Not going to treat us to another song this evening?"

"I've other games I want to play." PJ hummed to herself. "A walk is just the thing."

"A walk to anywhere in particular?"

"Maybe somewhere quiet. Somewhere warm and comfortable?" She leaned in just a little closer before pulling back. "Any suggestions?"

"A few." Aroha finished the last of her ale for a bit of clarity. She caught the draped lace sleeve of PJ's jacket, using it to pull her towards the exit. "Let's go."

With what felt like the weight of the entire village's gaze on them, Aroha led the way through the crowd and out of the pub. She ignored Rosa's thumbs-up and the Jain twins' winks. Gossip in South Myrddin would be rampant overnight; everyone would know by the morning that she'd gone for a "walk" with the wandering bagpiper.

Aroha enjoyed the brisk breeze that smacked her in the face the second they stepped outside. It helped cool her flushed face. "Maybe a walk through the park before we go somewhere… quieter?"

"I'm surprised my twin coppers didn't warn you off." PJ strolled along beside her. There was a fluidity to her movements—not quite a slither or a dance, yet more akin to both than a simple walk.

Aroha blinked a few times, once again having been mesmerised by her. "They did warn me about your preference for casual fun."

"And you still accepted my invitation?"

"Romance and romantic love have never been of interest to me." Aroha had, in the past, been judged by some for it. She'd never sought the deeper romantic connection so many around her seemed to crave. "I have always enjoyed fun."

"You dance to your own drum."

"And you sway to your own pipes." Aroha shook her head with a wry laugh. "That sounded far better in my head."

"I do indeed sway to the music of my pipes." PJ dashed in front of her, turning and bowing low with a twinkle in her eyes. Her laughter was a low, melodic sound that vibrated pleasantly through Aroha. "Good with my lips, my hands, and my hips."

"Are you now?"

"I am." PJ stood back up straight. She hooked a finger in one of the bracelets dangling from Aroha's wrist, tugging lightly until there was barely a sliver of space between them. "Perhaps I can show you?"

"Perhaps you can." Aroha rolled her arm until she had a hold of PJ's hand. She picked up the pace, leading her up the lane towards her shop and the privacy of the flat above it. "I'm eagerly anticipating the experience."

They barely made it into the shop before their lips connected in the first of many hungry kisses. A trail of fabrics and chains laid a path up to Aroha's bedroom. She was honestly surprised they made it.

The wreckage of their night of pleasure was laid bare in the dim light of a Scottish morning. A broken vase on the carpet—that she thought her elbow had caught. The little table by the bedroom door was on the floor, a victim of PJ's hips. Her body ached most deliciously.

Aroha lifted her head from the pillow, unsurprised to find PJ had already left. A steaming mug of coffee was on her nightstand with a note and a single rose, one of the magical varieties which bloomed all year round.

What a night.

What a woman.

It was honestly a relief to wake up alone. Aroha had never enjoyed pillow talk the morning after a satisfying night. It often led to feelings—ones she had never been able to return.

After taking a moment to stretch languidly on her silk sheets, Aroha forced herself to sit up. She grabbed the coffee and sipped slowly. The note was sweet and to the point.

You are certainly an unclouded light, offering me a brilliant view of the stars at night. Perhaps we can enjoy each other again another evening. For now, I'll dance to my own tune in another place. PJ

Aroha tossed the note aside and picked up the rose, bringing it to her nose to enjoy the sweet, floral scent. *What a perfect night.*

Gossip, Aroha had no doubts, would be flowing around the village. Someone had to have seen PJ leave unless she'd slithered away as a serpent. All of the gentle teasing was undoubtedly worth the aggravation for how incredibly and intensely sated she felt in body and spirit.

Aroha had barely had time to get out of bed and pull on her robe when someone rang the bell to the shop. She went over to peer out the window, immediately spotting Rosa below, who waved at her. "It's too early."

"I have fresh coffee and pastissets de boniato."

"The normal version or your extra-spiced version?" Aroha had a weakness for the sweet fried pastries made with a delicious sweet potato filling. Rosa had a spiced version that was like no other—one of her many culinary experiments.

"Mine, of course." She lifted the tray in her arms. "Can I come up, or should I see if someone else wants them?"

"You just want to hear the juicy gossip first."

"I'm willing to pay for the pleasure." Rosa grinned unrepentantly. "Are you going to open up?"

"Yes, yes." Aroha left the window open to let some fresh air into her flat. She rushed down into the shop to allow Rosa inside. "There's not much juicy gossip to share."

"So, I didn't see a familiar Pied Piper leaving your place before dawn while I was taking a delivery from the farm." Rosa followed her into the flat and set the tray on the coffee table. She plopped onto the sofa before reaching over to pick up something from the floor. "Not where you usually keep your necklaces. How wild *was* your night?"

Aroha refused to blush. She snatched the necklace and shoved it into the pocket of her robe. "No idea how that got there."

"None? None at all? I'm sure I can imagine a few ways it might've arrived on the floor." Rosa smirked when Aroha glowered at her. "Have some coffee."

"Fine." She grabbed one of the mugs and a pastry, sitting on the sofa beside Rosa. "I honestly have no memory of the necklace coming off."

"Or the shirt dangling from the bookshelf?"

Aroha kicked herself for not grabbing it when she'd gone to open the door. "Nope."

"That good of a night?"

"Best I can remember in recent history." Aroha left out that "recent history" was longer than she would've liked. It had been a long drought. "I'm sure you don't want the details."

"I can tell. Your hair is a mess, and I'm fairly certain you have a few marks to prove it." Rosa pointed towards her neck. "There's a lovely line of them. Like a necklace made of pleasure instead of metal. Where's your brush? I'll braid your hair for you."

Knowing her friend well enough, Aroha decided

not to argue. She meandered slowly into her bedroom, munching on a pastry while hunting for a brush or comb. She finally found one underneath a shirt on top of her dresser.

Rosa had moved to the arm of the couch, motioning for Aroha to sit in front of her. She took the brush from her and began to gently run it through her hair. "So, was the snake charming?"

Aroha reached around to flick her friend on the leg. "That was terrible."

"But accurate?" Rosa swatted Aroha's hand with the brush when she went to flick her for the second time. "Behave yourself."

"You first."

They both giggled before settling down. Shifters and vampires didn't often make the greatest of friends outside the village, but South Myrddin tended to be a law unto itself. The two had been friends almost since Aroha arrived. Rosa had been here longer, and her bakery was already an established shop. She'd been a great help when it came to opening up Unclouded Light.

"Do you think…?" She trailed off, unable to put thought to her fears.

"What? Tell me." Rosa had finally finished brushing out her hair and began to carefully braid it. She had a light, delicate touch that was almost putting Aroha to sleep. "Something wrong?"

"No, not really." Aroha tried to gather her thoughts. She sipped her coffee and then set the mug to the side. "It's just… PJ is the first to be so open about her preferences when it comes to casual connections instead of searching for some deep, abiding love."

"I've told you before there's nothing wrong with you. You like who you like—and you prefer what you prefer. There's no shame in it."

"There's an entire collection of novels, movies, and music that would disagree."

"And those aren't meant for you. They're for people who do experience romantic love. They aren't an indictment on your being aromantic—or they shouldn't be. It's not an essential part of the experience of being alive. You aren't… missing a part of yourself. It is simply who you are. " Rosa had always been adamant about it whenever Aroha had a rare moment of self-doubt. "I'm glad you had fun."

"I did."

"There." Rosa finished the last of the braid, making sure to secure it carefully. "Prepare yourself for a healthy dose of village curiosity. Everyone saw you two leaving the pub."

"Everyone?"

"Well, not everyone in the known universe, but certainly in the village." Rosa was utterly unaffected by Aroha's dramatic groan. "One shouldn't waltz out of a pub with a beautiful woman on their arm if one doesn't want to be the source of gossip for the next morning."

"One doesn't, does one?"

Rosa responded in the most adult-like manner possible by sticking her tongue out. "I spent the past twenty minutes on the phone with my uncle. He brings out the worst in me."

"He's mellowed some."

"As mellow as he can be." Rosa waved her hand as if to shake off the spectre of Detective Chief Inspector Pacheco. "He's been spending more time with Emrys."

"Has he?" Aroha shifted down the couch to allow her friend to move off the arm of the sofa. "How very intriguing."

"Not intriguing enough for everyone to forget you disappeared with the Pied Piper."

"Why are we friends?" She let her head fall back against the cushions with a tired groan. "I don't even care about the gossip. Last night was worth it."

"Yeah?"

"Yes, definitely," Aroha answered without hesitation. "She was worth it."

The End

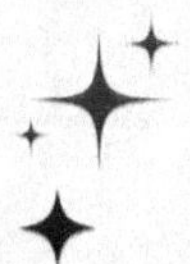

SNAPSHOTS OF A FADED AFFAIR

From awkward, almost sweet beginning to bitterly icy end, Emrys and Jonatan Pacehco can never seem to forget each other. If soulmates were fated, their bond has to be cursed. Despite a gulf of time and pain between them, it is nigh impossible for them to say goodbye.

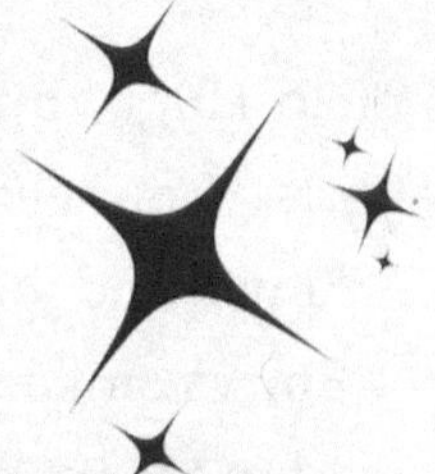

SNAPSHOT: A FIRST MEETING

EMRYS

A shout drew his attention from foraging in the woods. A cry followed by a ponderance of splashing. Emrys rushed out of the thicket of trees to the nearby bridge. It crossed over one of the inlets that fed into the sea.

The vision that greeted him gave him a moment of pause. He had to collect himself, blinking a few times to ensure he hadn't hallucinated. Meditation in the woods occasionally gave him visions, after all.

A tall man clung to one of the piers just barely out of the water. One of the largest trout Emrys had ever seen had a hold of his cloak. The fish was so large it had to be a shifter.

It *was* a shifter. Emrys thought he knew exactly which one as well. He wondered what the vampire had done to anger the trout.

"Ho there. Are you needing a hand?" Emrys tried

not to laugh, but it burst out of him despite his best efforts. "You seem to have made a friend."

"I will end you."

Emrys smiled while leaning on his staff. "You sure you don't want help?"

The trout wiggled wildly on the vampire's cloak, dislodging him from the pier. Both fell back into the water with a mighty splash. Emrys didn't even attempt to hold back his laughter this time; he indulged for a moment before striding forward to help the stranger.

"Ease off him, Mac. He won't taste good. Vampires are all ash and blood." Emrys pushed the fish off the stranger, and it immediately shifted into a short, angry, old barnacle of a man. "Go on with you. I'll deal with him."

"Fine." Mac stomped his way to the shore and disappeared in moments.

"I've never known if Mac was short for mackerel. I almost hope it is for the sheer irony." Emrys sighed when the vampire glowered at him. He didn't offer his hand as he introduced himself. "I haven't seen you before. Your face is familiar."

The vampire ripped off his cloak while stalking out of the water onto the shore. He wrung out what seemed like an endless stream of murky water. Emrys wasn't clear if his grimace of distaste was over the state of his clothing or his presence.

"Jonatan Pacheco." He didn't extend his hand either.

"Ah. The heir apparent to the coven of covens." Emrys had heard a new leader was rising amongst the vampires. His run-ins with them tended to end spikily. Druids and fae, of which he was both, tended to bring out the worst in the fanged ones. A careful balance had kept a semblance of peace between the various races in Scotland. "What brings you out to the wilds of Scotland? Here to sneer at the unworthy as your kind is wont to do?"

"Are all druids so suspicious and bitter?"

Emrys tapped his staff on the ground. It resonated with the magic of the land, swirling around them and rising like a heavy pressure on the soul. "I am cautious, not bitter. Vampires like to rule from high places. This isn't your domain. Keep your fangs away from South Myrddin."

"Or?"

"I will wear them around my neck as a warning to others. The village is mine to keep safe." Emrys cared for each foundling who called the village home. He'd sworn to protect them as he had been. "If you mean those I love harm, I will return the favour tenfold."

"So very unwelcoming."

"You are welcome to call the Highlands home so long as you remember the only ones you rule are your own kind." Emrys allowed the haze of anger to fade and got a decent look at Pacheco. He was handsome and well-dressed, though his appearance had been mired by his encounter with fish and river. His eyes were striking. It gave Emrys pause. "I offer a warning only, not a threat. One I'd make to warlock, witch, shifter, or vampire."

"After you went to the trouble of wading into a river for me?" Pacheco finished messing with his cloak and draped it over his arm. "I mean your foundlings no harm. You may not believe me, but I wish to protect this place. It speaks to me more than my home ever has."

"You haven't answered why you are here." Emrys followed him further up the embankment away from the water. They wound up on the bridge itself. "Is there a blood banquet? A liquid feast?"

"How very droll." Pacheco left a muddy trail in his wake as he walked over to stare out towards the raging sea in the distance. "The warlocks have been causing havoc of late in more places than the Highlands. They are drifting further south each year. Someone has to stop them. The druids seem uninterested in doing so. You must surely see they have to be curtailed."

The vampire had a point. Emrys had worried for a while over the trouble with the warlocks. Individual warring factions who came together to destroy everything in their path.

Vampires wanted control. Druids aimed for balance. But warlocks? They craved chaos and destruction.

Once, they'd been content to wield their magic and build their fortresses. Now, new leaders had risen who wanted to conquer. Emrys had watched the growing problem, knowing he'd be forced to intervene eventually.

"Your silence speaks loudly."

"Does it? About as useful as a fart in the wind, I imagine, since you've no idea what is going on in my mind." Emrys stepped up beside Pacheco. He was by no means a short man, but Pacheco stood even taller. His wet clothes clung to his body in very attractive ways that Emrys tried to ignore. "I've heard rumblings of trouble."

"We could work together."

"Vampires and druids?" Emrys had rarely seen them coexist without quarrel, let alone do something constructive. "The last time I attempted to do anything even close to helpful with one of your kind, they called me a shrivelled old mushroom."

"Rich coming from a fellow vampire." Pacheco's stormy blue eyes penetrated his soul when he glanced towards Emrys. "I wouldn't call you shrivelled or old.

There is, however, always a faint whiff of herb and forest about a druid."

"I've been called worse." Emrys trusted a vampire nose for scent better than his own. "Vampires will only enrage the warlocks."

"We are strong enough to handle them."

"I will *not* have my Highlands turned into a forever battlefield between factions." Emrys gripped his staff tightly in his hands. "My foundlings will not become caught up in the crossfire between you."

"You are protective over your charges."

"I was once one of them." Emrys had never forgotten the pain of those early years before Myrddin had found him and created a safe oasis for him. It fuelled his obsession with keeping the village safe and welcoming. "We protect our own—our family. The only ones to claim us."

They walked in silence for a moment. Emrys pondered the mystery of the tall vampire with a slight Spanish lilt to his voice. He was oddly drawn to Pacheco, which surprised him greatly.

"We could help each other." Pacheco seemed surprised at having made the offer. "I imagine the warlocks, with or without vampire interference, will turn their attention to your village eventually."

"I'd like to see them try." Emrys knew Myrddin had woven powerful protection into the land itself. "It would take far more than a pack of warlocks to breach the boundary."

"Still, it would be easier to deal with the problem before it becomes a more dire situation. Not even the famed protections of the greatest druid to live can keep them out forever." Pacheco turned around, leaning against the wall. He crossed his arms and looked far more dignified than he should, considering the mess of his clothing. "They will only grow in power."

"I am not eager to hand over control of the Highlands to vampires."

"You'd prefer the warlocks?" Pacheco held his hands up when Emrys raised his staff. "I am not making threats or speaking empty words. They will not stop until they control or ruin everything. It is their way."

"And vampires are better?"

"We're not seeking to rule the Highlands."

Emrys leaned heavily on his staff. He peered off into the distance, listening to the waves crashing and distant cry of one of his falcons. "No, you simply wish to bleed us dry."

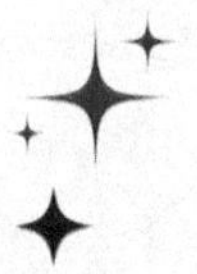

SNAPSHOT: A FIRST KISS

JONATAN

In a matter of months, Jonatan had settled himself in the Highlands. His family coven had a comfortable and impressive estate near the coast. It was practically a fortress—and an easy distance to several villages.

Time had flown by since his arrival. More vampires had been drawn further and further north in Scotland. The Pachecos had maintained control over the various other family covens, which helped him ease growing concerns amongst the druids at least. Nothing seemed to satisfy the warlocks.

They hungered for power and control—craved it. Jonatan had grown concerned about the way they delved deeper and deeper into forbidden magic. Warlocks had long since kept themselves in check; he feared what might happen if they stopped.

The warlocks were definitely becoming a problem.

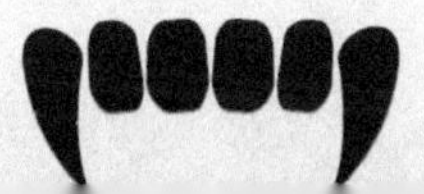

Insidious pests. He had hoped to talk sense with some of the noble families, but a revolution of sorts appeared to be happening. It was difficult to determine a leader amidst the chaos.

Jonatan stalked out of his bedroom. He might run into Emrys. It had become something of a weekly ritual. They met in secret to avoid issues with his family, sharing tea and conversation. *I wonder if he has a new herbal blend for us to try.*

It was never intentional—that's what they said. Their "accidental" meetings in the same place at almost the same time. The lies they conjured to make themselves feel better about the growing connection.

He told himself their chats were a means to an end. It had nothing to do with his enjoyment of Emrys's company. Vampires had standards, something his father had repeated to him over the years.

One didn't indulge baser desires when one was a Pacheco.

His father and grandfather had laid out the guidelines for the future of their coven—of all the covens. The Pachecos had clung to power for centuries. It had been drilled into him from an early age—protect the family name, reputation, and history.

He paused in front of a mirror to adjust his hair and the collar of his shirt. The weight of responsibility had always been a heavy burden. His grandfather had been particularly overbearing about it; his grandmother had taught him to guard his heart.

At some point, Jonatan would marry and continue the family line. That had been his father and grandfather's plan. They refused to allow some offshoot of the Pachecos to gain control.

Perhaps Emrys had been right in his assessment of vampires. They clung to power. Jonatan had lived long enough to see how it could all go wrong, so he understood the obsession.

Still.

And still.

A small part of his heart wondered if there might be a different future for him. They had long lives, almost immortal ones. Strength that lasted centuries, allowing his father to be at the helm of their coven and *all* covens for a long time.

Perhaps too long.

Emrys had been an unexpected fly in the ointment. Jonatan couldn't deny a growing attraction to the druid, no matter how hard he tried. It was a distraction. One he could ill afford at a time when the warlocks were becoming an increasing issue. They had quieted a little as the vampires reclaimed territory for themselves, likely trying to assess this new threat.

Making his way out of the house, Jonatan considered shadowing away, but he needed something else. A distraction to shake off some of the restless energy building inside him. Maybe a ride on horseback would work out all of his pent-up frustration. He snapped his fingers, and one of the lesser vampires who worked the estate rushed over.

Control had been a hallmark of the Pacheco family. Yet he couldn't ignore the way Emrys had brightened up his world. His voice was a liquid heat that seemed to flow through his body, setting him alight.

"Thank you." Jonatan nodded, taking the reins of the horse brought to him. He climbed into the saddle with ease and allowed the magnificent beast to canter forward.

On the mornings when Jonatan rode, he had a specific path in mind, another part of his regimented routine. The move to Scotland had forced him to create a new one. Each day, he'd found it shifting ever so slightly.

He had initially stuck to the estate's grounds but now found himself straying to the same place. And somehow, he always veered off towards the wild woods where druids were wont to walk. It was as if he weren't fully in control of himself, something he'd never experienced before in his life.

When Jonatan inevitably ran into Emrys, they argued and threw pointed barbs at each other. A strange sort of courtship. Yet they always found themselves returning. He sternly reminded himself it wasn't a romantic connection.

They were… friends of a sort.

It could never be anything more. He had responsibilities to his family—to his kind. None of them involved Emrys.

None of them should involve Emrys.

"Does your family know where these rides take you?" Emrys sat on a stonewall further down the path with his staff resting against it. "Vampires, in my experience, are usually eager to avoid my company. Something about the nature of my power. Perhaps it reminds them that no heart beats in their chest."

"Maybe it's simply you that they find distasteful?"

"I can't imagine why. You don't seem repulsed." Emrys stretched a hand out, and much to Jonatan's annoyance, his horse immediately walked forward to greet him. "Most creatures enjoy my company."

"Again, I can't imagine why."

"I am surprised to see you on horseback so often. I've always thought vampires enjoyed showing off their power through the speed of movement or simply travelling through shadow." Emrys spent a moment greeting his horse. "He's a wonderful beast. Powerful. I can see what draws you to him."

"There's a freedom to riding." Jonatan found himself being more open than he'd usually be. He tended to keep things close to the chest. "A shared moment between the horse and myself. Nothing can disrupt it, no matter how brief it may be."

"Heavy is the head who carries the weight of family history and reputation?"

"The warlocks have grown quiet." Jonatan was eager to move the conversation away from his family. "Do you believe it will last?"

"Neither of us is naïve enough for that. We both know once one steps onto a path of sacrifice for power, it is a rare thing to avoid the never-ending siren's call." Emrys reached for his staff as he hopped off the wall. "The quiet cannot last, though I wish it otherwise. I have added layers of protection to South Myrddin."

"The quiet never lasts." Jonatan slid from the saddle. He walked forward, trying not to smile when Emrys fell in step with him. The horse followed behind them. "I once dreamed of a career in law, helping protect others, whether as a barrister or taking up a seat in parliament. I wanted to make a difference."

"A lofty goal."

"For a vampire?" He couldn't help needling Emrys. "We don't all crave power or control."

"A lofty goal for anyone. What stopped you?"

"I have a duty to my family." Jonatan had spent many years in preparation for his goal and then been forced to throw it all away. His obligations were always going to clash with his hopes for the future. "We are ready if the warlocks decide to become a problem for the Highlands."

"When, not if." Emrys stopped walking and leaned on his staff. "Our paths keep crossing. I almost think you seek me out."

"A coincidence—nothing more, nothing less." Jonatan kept his gaze on the fields in the distance. He could never admit the truth to Emrys. It would be a fool's errand. "We could offer protection for your village."

"At what cost? I will not cede control over it to anyone."

Jonatan couldn't blame him. In times of the past, vampires had, in essence, conquered territories and held them. "We don't rule with an iron fist."

"Or a wooden stake?" Emrys smiled in the face of Jonatan's glower. "The Highlands won't cower in the face of anyone. We'd sooner make a bonfire out of your grand estate."

"A threat?"

"A promise."

One second, they were threatening death by flames. The next, Emrys had him pressed against the stone wall. A single forbidden kiss. It was addictive; one moment burned into the next until something pressed between them.

"What…?" Jonatan drew away from Emrys as his horse pushed between them. He tried to shake off the feeling of their kiss. All thoughts of tea had vanished. "I should return to the estate."

"Jonatan."

"Good day."

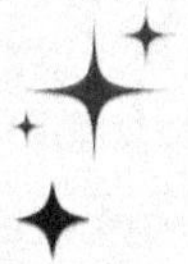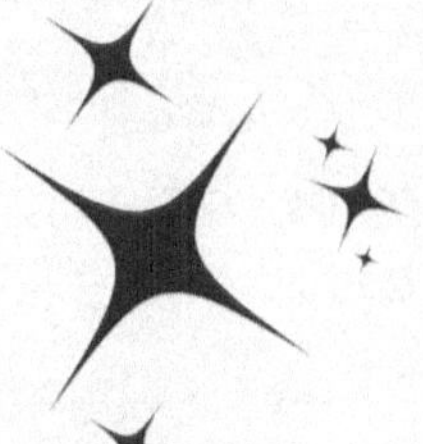

SNAPSHOT: A TRYST IN THE FORREST

EMRYS

Months had passed since that first kiss. Emrys hadn't seen or heard anything from the vampire. It wasn't a surprise; he told himself he wasn't disappointed.

His time was taken up with village life. They were rebuilding one of the cottages at the edge of South Myrddin. It had been empty for years and had gotten damaged in a recent wild winter storm.

While South Myrddin had no official mayor, he shared the role of leader with the heads of the witch coven and the village pack comprised of werewolves and shifters. He filled his time with it, avoiding thoughts of a tall vampire and a searing kiss.

The rebuild kept his mind busy. Emrys also avoided straying into the woods, where he'd be more likely to run into Jonatan. He was too old to play the lovestruck fool.

Today, however, it couldn't be avoided. He had made his way through the fields to his preferred wooded area outside the village. A sacred place where he had laid an altar, one that had served him well for nigh on a century or more.

It was a beautiful day. The wild woods called to him. Emrys followed the pull as he always had, listening to what the land wanted of him.

The sea was close enough for the scent of salty air to mingle with the heavy aroma of the cherry and pine trees. No matter the season, things grew underfoot in the middle of the forest. A heady perfume to over-whelm the senses of any druid. He stood, steps away from his altar, tilting his head back and breathing deeply.

He sensed a change in the woods, a warning of an intruder. "Finished hiding?"

"I wasn't hiding."

"You were." Emrys lowered his head and tilted his staff, twisting around to find an oddly hesitant Jonatan. "Playing coward doesn't suit you."

"I am no coward."

"No?" Emrys allowed the magic of the glade to dance around him. He could also see Jonatan was affected by it from the way his eyes darted around, expecting something tangible in the air. "You've been hiding from this—from us."

"There is no us."

Emrys thought "there can be no us" might be a more accurate sentiment. "Yet here you are. You've brought yourself into the woods to find me."

"A sheer coincidence."

"Lying to yourself as well as running away to hide? How very disappointing," Emrys teased, forcing himself to adopt a light tone. He rested his elbow on top of his staff, half expecting Jonatan to stomp off. "You could simply accept the growing attraction—the desire bubbling up between us like a potion in a cauldron. If left untouched, it may very well burn us."

Jonatan stalked towards him. He grasped Emrys by the loose folds of his cloak, dragging him forward until nothing separated their lips but a breath. "This will end badly."

"As do most of my experiments. Why stop the trend now?" Emrys laughed wildly, only to be silenced by a rough kiss.

"If you were anything other than a druid, I'd claim to have been bewitched," Jonatan murmured. His lips found Emrys's in a second searing taste. "Maybe this will get you out of my mind."

"Or make it worse." Emrys drew him deeper into the woods. Here, the magic of the earth was wild and pure. It flooded through him and welcomed him as always, setting him alight much as the kiss had done. "Nothing says we cannot indulge."

"My family has expectations."

"Do you often bring your family into bedchamber conversations?" Emrys smirked. He dragged his fingers down Jonatan's chest. "Nothing but a canopy of trees and a few ravens above us. They'll never tell our secrets."

The forest protected him. It had always been his sanctuary before South Myrddin had even existed. He had no doubts it would continue to do so even in the face of a forbidden romance.

A feverish desire took over both of them. Clothes were stripped, naked want blatantly clear between them. Emrys surrendered to the flow of lust that carried them away to a carnal haze.

Time passed. Emrys had no idea how much had gone, so deep in the forest and sated to the point of exhaustion. He lay on the soft ground in front of his altar with a dozing vampire at his side; there was no denying their connection now.

As they recovered, Emrys found his thoughts drifting to other things. His mind latched onto a problem he'd been considering for months. The warlocks. Their prolonged quiet had a worrying nature to it.

"Castle MacDougal sits in a powerful and historic

location. One the warlocks have begun making subtle moves towards." Emrys sat up slowly. He fixed his shirt and retied his breeches. "I've heard rumblings of Codrin cel Mare coming to the Highlands within the year or maybe next to soothe tensions with the warlocks."

"How will he help?"

"Codrin the Great? He of the principality of Moldavia," Emrys continued. Jonatan gave an elegant shrug. "One of the few, if not the only, living members of a noble warlock family—a royal one at that."

"Odd he would come here."

"My thoughts exactly until I considered warring factions may be opening up." Emrys didn't know if Codrin's appearance would help or hurt matters.

"Your sweet nothings leave something to be desired." Jonatan lingered beside him as they finished redressing themselves. Emrys had expected him to bolt. "Must we speak of warlocks now?"

Emrys climbed to his feet and brushed off his clothing. He smothered a chuckle at the almost pouting vampire, who appeared to be meticulously plucking debris from his cloak. "You'll want a dip in the lake if you're hoping to avoid anyone noticing we've... indulged. Scent lingers, after all."

"We cannot do this again." Jonatan continued picking at his clothing, straightening and brushing off his cloak. He fastidiously messed with his hair. "I have no regrets."

"Good to know." Emrys stepped forward, smirking as he plucked a small twig from Jonatan's collar. "Surely this isn't the end of the world."

"Perhaps not for the average vampire and druid. We are *not* average." Jonatan flicked a leaf off his cloak. He finally stopped fussing with his clothing and met Emrys's bemused gaze. "I have no regrets."

"I heard you the first time." Emrys remained unbothered. He had no expectations to hinder him from seeking pleasure. As long as he was happy, the ones he considered family would be thrilled for him. "We will see each other again, I have no doubts."

"I...." Jonatan took a step back and then disappeared into shadow.

"Coward." Emrys chuckled. "You'll be back."

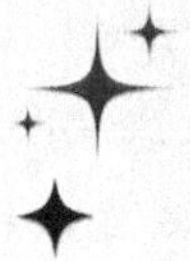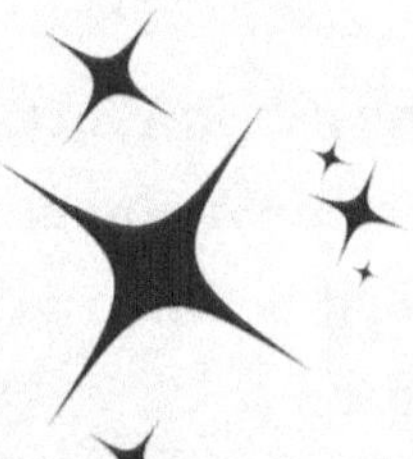

SNAPSHOT: LOVE IS A BATTLEFIELD

JONATAN

In the blink of an eye, a decade had passed. Jonatan had seen the rise and fall of the warlocks, the ruination of Castle MacDougal, and the fleeing of those who inhabited it to the fae realm. It had been a chaotic ten years.

He had no emotional ties to Ness MacDougal and her lovers. Their flight to the fae had provided the perfect opportunity to rout the warlocks. Those who remained had essentially gone into hiding instead of facing the ire of every living being in the Highlands.

His relationship with the wild-haired druid had continued, much to his bewilderment. His body had a mind of its own. He could never seem to call to a halt his liaison with Emrys.

They had gone from trysts in the woods to travelling together and spending long nights before the

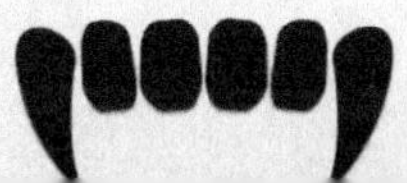

hearth in Emrys's cottage. He regularly told himself it meant nothing. A small lie. The tiniest of prevarications that he often feared would eventually cost him a great deal.

His grandfather and father had both tired of life in the Highlands. They'd returned home to Spain with the majority of the family, leaving him in control of the various vampire covens in Scotland and the estate. It had felt like another sign that he should end his extended fling with Emrys.

And yet he had been unable to bring himself to stop. It had also seemed a sign from the universe to continue, since any who might protest were no longer in the country. He had become far too emotionally attached to the druid.

Taking the reins of the covens had come surprisingly easy to him. Jonatan had expected to chafe under the weight of responsibility. He thrived, or at least, that was his perspective.

The issue with the warlocks had given him a greater understanding of the Highlands. He grasped now why Emrys had cautioned him about the vampires' approach to the area. While he maintained control over his own people, it had been made clear that was the extent of his power.

It had been several months since Jonatan had seen his lover. He'd tried to put some space between them.

They were becoming too attached; he couldn't shake the feeling that things couldn't continue on as they were.

Something had to change.

He, like many of the Pachecos, was slow to change. It would've made a fitting family motto. *We, the ones who are more tortoise than hare.* He supposed it didn't have a regal or powerful ring to it.

"Going riding?"

Jonatan nodded to the vampire who ran the farmland and stables. He had been one of the few who remained behind when his family returned to Spain. "It's been too long."

Promising himself to remain on their land, Jonatan quickly found himself breaking his word. He allowed the horse to follow the familiar path across the pastures, over a fence, and onto the lane leading to dangerous places. It somehow didn't surprise him when Emrys awaited as if he'd been there for days.

"You've been avoiding me again." Emrys sat on the familiar stone boundary to his wooded sanctuary. "Was it something I said?"

Jonatan couldn't help wondering if Emrys had indeed been there waiting for days on end. Or perhaps the merlin falcons he used as a messenger had alerted him to an intruder. "I haven't been avoiding you."

"You have."

"I have responsibilities." Jonatan knew his oft-repeated excuse sounded weak. "You surely see we cannot continue as we once were."

"And yet you brought yourself here. Why? For one last taste?" Emrys was maddeningly unbothered by all of it. "You play far too coy for a vampire of your age. We're not teething toddlers in the first flush of young love."

Jonatan seethed internally, not wanting to reveal how conflicted he'd been. If anything, he longed for Emrys to be at least somewhat visibly affected by the quagmire of indecision. "I am responsible for all of the covens in the isles. This is a distraction."

"Not the worst thing I've been called in my life." Emrys stood on the stone wall with his staff at his side. He seemed almost majestic, particularly when one of his falcons landed on his shoulder. "Would it be so wrong to admit to caring about each other? Whether carnal or otherwise, there is nothing shameful in love."

"If I fail to meet expectations, someone else will be given control over the covens." Jonatan clenched the reins tightly in his hands. "Neither of us wants that to happen. I care about this area. Maybe I don't have the connection you have, but it has become important."

"I haven't asked for your hand in marriage." Emrys waited until the falcon took flight, then leapt off the wall. He strode forward and patted the neck of

Jonatan's horse, murmuring soothingly to him. "Why must vampires be so dramatic? Flouncing off in a puff of smoke. If you are the head that wears the fanged crown, you should act like it. Who's going to judge you now?"

"If there were a crown, I'd be head of all—not just the vampires."

"You'd look pretty with a crown." Emrys took a step back from the horse. "Why are you here?"

"I...."

"While I enjoy a tryst as much as anyone does, I am not a toy to be yanked to and fro." Emrys held a hand up to stop Jonatan when he opened his mouth to speak. "We are both adults who went into this with eyes wide open. The horse didn't bring you here of its own free will. You hold the reins."

"Emrys."

"I've never minded a secret affair. I do, however, find uncertainty to be tiresome. Do you want to seek pleasure or not?" Emrys shook his head when Jonatan continued to mentally flounder. "Vampires. Enjoy your position. You might find it a lonely one."

Without another word, Emrys spun around and strode off. He made quite the vision when a falcon once again landed on his shoulder. Jonatan watched until he'd disappeared into the mist surrounding the forest.

The image of Emrys was burned into his mind. A riot of shoulder-length greying hair was partially hidden beneath his heavy green-hooded cloak. With the gnarled, hand-carved staff in his hand and the falcon on his shoulder, he looked every inch the powerful druid with ancient fae blood.

"I should follow." Jonatan grasped the reins tightly before tugging on them, guiding his horse to turn around. Maybe it was better this way. "Home. Time to go home."

Maybe he would regret this decision. But he couldn't live his life torn between responsibility and desire. He had always put his family first; it wouldn't do to stop now.

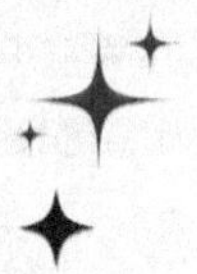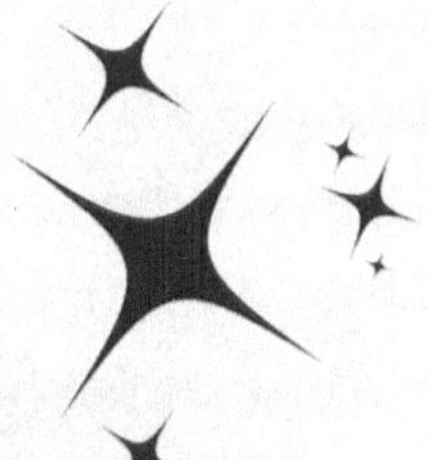

SNAPSHOT: DEVOID OF HOPE

EMRYS

Almost a century had flown by. Emrys stuck to his decision but still found a way to gain some amusement from it. He refused to pretend they hadn't known each other intimately and carnally, something Jonatan seemed insistent on doing.

The great detective.

While a police force had existed in Scotland since the 1600s, detectives were new to the nineteenth century. It wasn't surprising when Jonatan became the Highlands' first detective inspector. He had been made for the position.

It seemed Jonatan had, in some small way, accomplished his dream. Yet he had also remained alone. He had never caved to pressure from his family to marry.

They saw each other every so often, and their relationship had initially been cordial. Emrys enjoyed

poking at the distinguished Detective Inspector Pacheco, though. A vampire who'd become even more obsessed with justice and having things in order.

In an order he preferred.

There were few glimpses of the Jonatan who'd so often ride down the lane to the wooded sanctuary. It was sad. He seemed to have erased or buried the parts of him that Emrys had fallen in love with.

"Admit it. You miss him." Emrys stared at his own reflection in the small water gathered in a bowl. He'd left it in the garden through the quiet moon of January. Finally, he flicked his fingers into it, dispelling the image of himself. "It's been over for ages. If you can't let him go, let him be."

While at the beginning, it had been nothing beyond physical attraction and satisfaction, feelings had developed between them. It didn't matter at this point, but he could, at least, acknowledge them to himself. Still, the relationship had ended many, many years ago.

In that time, South Myrddin had continued to grow. They had a thriving farm, orchard, and fishery around the village. New shops and cottages sprang up all the time. They had welcomed several foundlings in the passing years.

There was plenty to distract himself.

Emrys touched his staff to the moon-blessed water, murmuring under his breath in a mixture of Gaelic and

Fae. Once he was finished, he poured it into a series of small jars for later use. His mind only partially focused on the task.

If we let each other go, why does he so often visit my dreams?

Carrying the bottles and bowl into the shed converted into a library and ritual space, Emrys busied himself. The distraction didn't work. He finally gave up and strode back into the garden.

The sun was beginning to make its presence known. He breathed in deeply and then released some of the tension. If he couldn't let Jonatan go, perhaps, if nothing else, he should let it be.

Unfinished business had never settled well with him. He preferred closure. Proper, definite closure. And it didn't help that he'd had so little control over the matter.

Making his way through the garden and around his cottage, Emrys decided to grab himself breakfast. He wanted to check on one of the new shops that had sprung up—a bakery that served custom tea blends. It would be the perfect thing to take his mind off things… or perhaps make things worse.

"Easy there, old man. Your brain will catch fire if you're not careful. All that heavy thinking."

Emrys sighed loudly. He turned to find who he considered to be the village annoyance sitting on the stone wall across from his cottage. "Bram."

"I've heard things."

"The wind whistling through your ears?" Emrys continued walking. He grumbled to himself when Bram leapt up to prance along the wall to his left. "What have you heard?"

"A certain dashing vampire is most perturbed by the latest addition to the village." Bram leapt gracefully from the wall and landed in front of him. "His own niece. His own flesh and blood coming to dance amongst we merry few."

"Bram. There is no 'we.' You're a wandering feral fae bard who latched onto South Myrddin." Emrys had never been quite sure why a member of the Unseelie Court had decided to plant himself amongst them. He'd made himself comfortable in the lighthouse just on the edge of the village by the sea. "Don't pretend to be hurt."

"I won't. I shall control my desire to prostrate myself and wail in agony."

"I'm grateful for the restraint. How goes the court?" Emrys realised Bram had no intentions of leaving him to his morning. He accepted whatever chaos was to be as they walked side by side. "Anything of concern?"

"Nothing that might affect the village. Despite what you think of me, I care about your foundlings. There's beauty and peace in this place, and I've no intentions of mucking that up." Bram pulled his guitar around from where it rested on his back and strummed a note. "I have heard a wonderful little rumour about a certain vampire. He, with the large stick rammed up his—"

"Bram."

"He is apparently bothered by his own niece choosing the village rather than the Pacheco estate." Bram played a jaunty tune, practically prancing along beside Emrys. "Perhaps the two of you could…?"

"Do nothing. Whatever we may have had, it's over. And it has been too long for it to change now." Emrys wrapped his sadness around him like a cloak. He shielded himself from it and released the emotions with a sigh and a whispered curse. "He made his position clear. And I have no intentions of trying to change his mind."

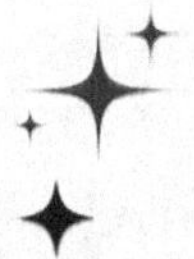

SNAPSHOT: NO GOOD ANSWERS

JONATAN

The call had come from his niece about a young vampire who'd been rumoured to be living alone. He had immediately gone to see if he could find them.

It had been a surprise to find out *who* the child was. The Snodgrasses were a family almost as ancient and powerful as his own. They had a tendency to be even more insular than his. He had never been fond of them.

Jonatan was sadly not surprised when his niece told him about the young vampire, though. He had, however, been furious. As both the coven leader and lead detective over the Highlands, he took personal offence to the abandonment of such a young child.

His first task had been to find the young one, and then he'd gone to confront their parents. In retrospect, he shouldn't have brought the child with him. He'd

just been so angry, and their excuses had only enraged him further.

Jonatan pinched the bridge of his nose. He pulled on all the patience he'd developed over the years in order to not rip the heads off the two vampires in front of them. "This is your child. Your only one. Your heir, in essence."

"No, we'll use my nephew. Phineas. He'll behave properly as a Snodgrass should."

Jonatan gritted his teeth at the disdain dripping from that single word. He felt the young vampire tense behind him. "You allowed—no, you *forced* them to fend for themselves at such an age."

"Our child refuses to fit in."

He felt like someone had punched him in the gut, remembering a starkly similar conversation happening with his sister a few decades earlier. "You may come to regret this."

"We won't."

Jonatan refused to waste another breath on them. He gently led the vampire out of the ostentatious house. He should probably have gotten their name sooner. "You don't have to see them again."

"What am I going to do?"

Jonatan wanted to offer comfort, but he'd never been skilled at that. He also didn't want to lie to them. "I know a village that welcomes foundlings."

"Foundlings?"

"Abandoned children. Can you tell me your name?" Jonatan placed a hand on the child's shoulder, preparing to shadow them to his estate for the moment. He'd need to speak to Emrys.

"I hate it."

"Well…." Jonatan was momentarily stumped. How did Emrys deal with the young so very easily? "You can choose another."

"Good."

Once the young Snodgrass was relatively comfortable at his estate, Jonatan made the journey to South Myrddin. As the years passed, Emrys remained mostly unchanged. His beard and hair had grown whiter, not that he seemed to care. He'd embraced the windswept fisherman look.

It looked good on him, not that Jonatan would ever admit it. Their chance had passed them by. Or perhaps, more truthfully, he had thrown it away.

To his family's eternal disappointment, Jonatan had never married or even glanced at any potential date they enjoyed throwing in his path. He wasn't interested. He had seen perfection; nothing else would ever compare.

"Jonatan." Emrys stood from where he'd been sitting in his garden, enjoying the late-afternoon sun and a pipe. "What brings you to my cottage? I know it isn't me."

He smothered a sigh and tried to appear unmoved by the mild barb tossed in his direction. "A foundling."

"We have many. The vast majority of the village is one."

"The Snodgrasses have abandoned one of their children." Jonatan had for the longest time assumed vampires were the exception to the foundlings, and then his own family had all but abandoned his niece. And now, he found yet another one on his hands. "I tried to intervene."

"And they didn't care?"

"I won't repeat what they said out of earshot, never mind the words they gleefully said in front of the child. I wouldn't trust them if they did recant." Jonatan hated feeling as though he'd failed one he considered part of his responsibility. "I'm sure Rosa mentioned them."

"She did."

Jonatan waited for more, but Emrys simply puffed on his pipe. *Damn him.* "The child deserves better."

"Agreed. Any foundling is welcome here." Emrys always seemed so effortlessly unaffected, while Jonatan constantly had to mask his feelings with a cool glare. "Do they have a name?"

"They said they hate it so… yes and no?" Jonatan

was completely out of his depth with the young Snodgrass. "Can you help?"

"Of course. Can you tell me anything about them? Rosa mentioned a love of reading and quietness." Emrys had seen all manner of foundlings over the years, Jonatan had no doubts his mind was already working on ways to help this one. "Do they have any belongings?"

"None on them save a few books. I plan to return to the Snodgrasses and see what I can salvage." Jonatan didn't like his chances. "When can I bring them?"

"Give me a day to get a place for them situated."

"Just like that?"

"You know how we are. If someone needs a home, we provide it for them." Emrys made his way through the garden towards the shed that was more of a tiny cottage than anything else. "They can stay here for a few days until we get more permanent accommodations figured out."

"I don't approve of what they're doing—abandoning their child."

"And yet you haven't punished them." Emrys opened the door to the shed, stepping inside and leaving Jonatan to follow. "Have you done anything about your niece aside from trying to convince her to conform to whatever impossible standards your family set for her?"

"I...."

"If you want to be a champion for justice, the one you dreamed of for so long, you have to do more than speak pretty words about it." Emrys made quick work of shelving books that were strewn about the small space. He pushed a table and chair into a corner and unfolded a cot. "It's more comfortable than it looks, particularly for a day or two."

"I am doing my best for all of the vampire covens."

"And what about those who don't fit so nicely into the box?" Emrys smiled knowingly when Jonatan had no answer for him. "One day, you'll have to contend with your inability to stand up for everyone."

"I brought them here." He'd instinctively known the village was a better place for the child.

"Aye, you did. I know you're doing your best, but hiding your heart behind an icy wall isn't smothering your ability to understand them—and us." Emrys's words cut too deeply. "I'll be here tomorrow. Bring your young Snodgrass with you. We'll take good care of them."

With a nod, Jonatan shadowed away. In many ways, it was the height of rudeness to simply vanish from within someone's home. He preferred to be outside before he did it.

As always, Emrys had cut him to the quick with a few words. A kind but brutal honesty that Jonatan couldn't hide from. He didn't head straight home, afraid of taking out his frustrations on an innocent, so he returned to the Snodgrass estate instead.

They were worthy targets of his ire. One of the younger Snodgrasses led Jonatan to where he'd saved clothes and books—items that had been intended to be destroyed.

Making his way back home, Jonatan found the young vampire hiding in the library. They had gathered a stack of books around them like a fortress. He had no idea how, but they seemed to be reading several at one time.

"Your cousin managed to salvage two bags of your things. Clothes and some books." Jonatan set them down outside the makeshift fort. "Has your thirst been sated? There's a variety available, though you may be too young for blood wine."

"Where can I sleep?"

"Vampires don't sleep."

"We don't *need* sleep, but naps are delightful." They hadn't so much as glanced in his direction, but he was relieved to at least see them conversing with him. "Have you tried one? It's nice to close your eyes and not move. Blankets are soft."

"I...." Jonatan had never felt so incredibly out of his depth. "There are beds. I'll have one prepared for you for this evening. Tomorrow, I'll take you to South Myrddin."

"Is that where Rosa lives?"

"It is."

"They'd welcome me?"

Jonatan ignored the pang in his heart and how wistful yet guarded the young vampire sounded. "They will. I'm going to take you to someone I've known for a long time. Emrys. He's a druid and part fae. Looks like an old fisherman. He's kind and has a large collection of books. He'll take good care of you."

They looked up finally; their startlingly clear gaze met his, then immediately shifted away. "I'd like that— having someone to look out for me."

"Good." Jonatan tried to push away the growing sense of failure. "I'll leave you to the books."

"What did I do wrong?"

He froze. Such a simple yet painful question. One his niece had also asked him. He hadn't known what to tell her, and he still had no great answer. "I don't believe you did anything wrong at all."

They frowned. It wasn't a strong or confident answer, but it was all he had. Silence followed him as he strode out of the library.

Sometimes, as coven leader, there were no good answers.

And today was one of those days.

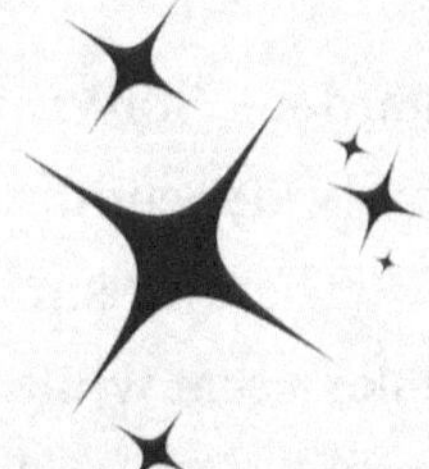

SNAPSHOT: FULL CIRCLE

EMRYS

It had been an exhausting end of the year. Emrys couldn't recall having so much turmoil in the village in the past. The only good thing was Jonatan had been drawn to South Myrddin repeatedly to deal with one murder after another.

After well over two centuries, Emrys had thought those feelings long buried. Yet it had all come rushing back. Everything they'd tried to ignore had become like a flash of light constantly shining above their heads.

As the moon rose over a new year, Emrys had spent the evening in his own garden. He'd left the celebrating to others. His mind was elsewhere.

"Emrys?"

He lowered the journal he'd been reading by firelight to find a somewhat subdued vampire in his

garden. "Jonatan. What are you doing out so late—or early, depending on how you look at it?"

There was no response. Emrys motioned for him to take a seat while he wandered into the cottage to grab a bottle of blood ale. He went back to the garden, offering it to Jonatan.

"Shall we toast to the coming year?"

"Slàinte Mhath." Jonatan lifted his ale in a toast.

"Do dheagh shlainte." Emrys tapped his bottle against Jonatan's. "And the good health to all those we care about as well."

"I saw Hyde in the park." Jonatan lowered himself into the chair beside Emrys's. He stretched his long legs out in front of him. "I was reminded of the day I brought them to your cottage."

"Oh?"

"They were braver than I realised at the time. They had the courage to be themselves and build a life they wanted." Jonatan sipped his ale for a moment before continuing. "It was a mistake to try to force them to conform—to try to bring them back into the coven. I thought they needed other vampires around them."

"It was." Emrys was surprised at the admission. Jonatan hadn't been so open in decades—centuries even. He'd thought that part of his former lover was buried and lost forever. "The village was the perfect place for Hyde. They might not have been so openly welcomed and encouraged anywhere else, certainly not with their supposed family."

A pleasant silence grew between them. Emrys waited patiently. Something had clearly happened to affect Jonatan, and he seemed to be struggling internally.

What had brought him to Emrys's door? They had been almost antagonistic with each other for such a long time. It had been painful to deal with at times when happier memories poked at him.

Sipping his own ale, Emrys reached out to add another log to the fire. He murmured a blessing and a prayer while focusing his intent on the flames. He had such hope for the future despite recent events in the village.

For a moment, Emrys could imagine what could have been between them while they sat in the garden. Decades together instead of centuries apart. It was an intoxicating vision of the past. He'd learned a long time ago that indulging those sorts of dreams was dangerous.

One had to live in the present—not the past.

It had been an age since the two of them simply enjoyed each other's company. Too often in recent years, they'd been at loggerheads, often over the best ways to help the foundlings, particularly the vampire ones. Emrys had been greatly relieved when

Jonatan had begun to adjust and let go of his expectations.

Emrys found himself carried away by the magic of the night and the warmth of the fire. He admitted something that he'd kept buried in his heart for an age. "I miss us—how we used to be."

The silence stretched between them. It felt weighted with the confession. Emrys was about to speak when Jonatan shifted in his chair.

"So do I."

"Then?" Emrys asked.

"I don't know how to find that man again." Jonatan took another sip of his drink. He glanced briefly at Emrys before focusing on the fire once again. "It feels as though a century of ice and stone have formed around me."

"You are fundamentally the same vampire I met all those years ago." Emrys felt as though he were tiptoeing across thin ice to reach a long-awaited prize. "Still the same longing for justice and the desire to protect, even if maybe you went about it the wrong way. Same handsome face with perhaps a little more grey than before."

"Isn't it too late for a rekindled romance?" Jonatan set his bottle of blood ale on the arm of the chair. He seemed mesmerised by the fire. "Where would we even start?"

"By the fire? A kiss as sweet as honey with no witnesses but the moon above us and without a risk of us murdering each other?" Emrys understood the hesitation… the trepidation. It was risky to tempt themselves after centuries apart. "You can't say our bond hasn't been forged in a flood of ancient history."

"Is that some sort of misguided confession?"

"Bram may have infected me with his special brand of prose. Our own feral wanderer." Emrys lifted his staff, tapping it against the ground. Lights immediately lit up through the branches above them. Music played from the old record player in the little shed. "Dance with me."

"Pardon?"

"Dance with me." Emrys set his staff down and got to his feet. "I promise I won't step on your toes."

"Emrys."

"Let me help you find yourself again." Emrys offered his hand to Jonatan, who drew himself up to his feet without help. "What's the worst that can happen?"

"Aren't we a little old for happily ever afters?"

"Who said anything about a happily ever after? I never enjoyed the phrase. It implies nothing ever happens again. We've seen the truth of the world—of magic and mayhem, both good and bad." Emrys slipped his hand into Jonatan's, strength meeting strength. "We're never too old to restart a romance. The question is… do you have the courage to try?"

Jonatan sighed. He dragged Emrys forward until their bodies were flush against each other. "For the sake of both of our toes, I'm leading. Just one dance."

"That's how it always starts."

The End

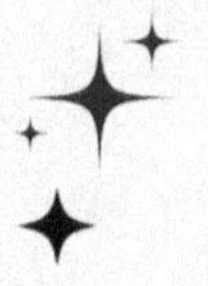 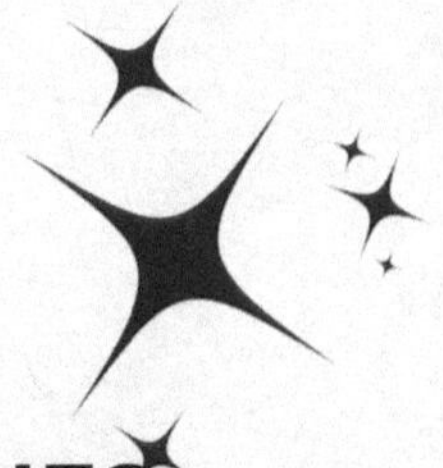

DELETED SCENES

A collection of short bits and pieces that don't quite fit into the series. See Hyde's arrival in the village and learn about Emrys's connection to the land. The chaos kittens make their very first appearance in their vampire's world.

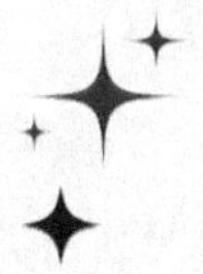

IN THE BEGINNING

EMRYS

His heart broke whenever a new foundling arrived. They were almost always skittish, and it reminded him far too much of his younger self. Each one took him back to the child druid abandoned by his kin.

No home.

No hope.

A lone druid with fae blood lost in the Highlands.

The last great mage, Myrddin, had found him, scrounging for any scrap of food and comfort. Emrys had been as weak as a fledgling falcon kicked from its nest too soon. He'd expected more pain, not the comfort offered to him.

Myrddin had taken him in and educated him, sharing his gift of magic. Most of all, he'd built a village for him. It had been a legacy and a duty placed on his shoulders.

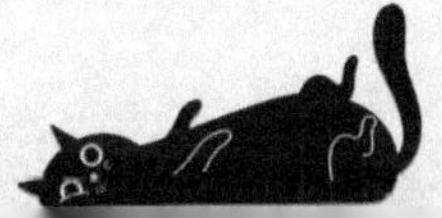

If Emrys closed his eyes, he could still see the humble beginnings of what they created. A single cottage grew stone by stone. Fae, druid, witch, dryad, vampire. South Myrddin had welcomed them all. It had felt, at the time, like overnight the village had sprung up out of the ether.

It hadn't. Blood, sweat, and tears had gone into its creation, along with a massive amount of Myrddin's power. The ancient mage had sacrificed a fair bit of himself to protect the land and those who chose to live there.

They'd fought for their small piece of Scotland. Hearth and home. A gift to any magical being and creature. He had never once forgotten the loneliness and fear from his youth. Everyone deserved to feel safe, welcomed, and loved.

Everyone.

Today would bring another newcomer to the village. A young vampire. Jonatan Pacheco, the vampire leader in Scotland, had reached out to him. A genuine surprise since they'd been avoiding each other for the past hundred years over a failed relationship and hurt feelings.

Jonatan had seemed genuinely upset when he mentioned a young one in need of a home. A Snodgrass, another surprise since they were one of the most insular vampire clans. They were the last family he'd thought would kick out one of their heirs.

Vampires rarely had more than one child. They tended to cherish their young. South Myrddin, as a result, rarely had the need to welcome one into their midst.

Jonatan hadn't told him much about the new foundling, which wasn't surprising. His former lover had a tendency to ignore the more personal aspects. He had a cold, calculated view of the world, though Emrys could admit to perhaps being biased when it came to seeing him clearly.

He did know the foundling was quiet. They loved to read, devouring books like a starving werewolf did steak. And they were young.

They had been abandoned outside the village. Pacheco, as vampire coven leader and a detective inspector with the police, had found them. He'd attempted reconciliation but quickly realised it was pointless.

They were still a child.

Far too young to be alone in the world.

In preparation for the arrival, Emrys had made up the living space in his garden library. It was small but would suffice until they got the foundling on their feet. He always preferred to give them time before finding them a place of their own.

Clothes could be bought. Books given. Things replaced. South Myrddin did one thing better than anything else: It allowed foundlings to build the life they wanted.

It was something Emrys cared a great deal about. They deserved the freedom to make choices and not have their lives directed and micromanaged. He'd fought and sacrificed a great deal of himself to do so.

"Emrys."

Emrys was pulled out of his thoughts by the painfully familiar voice. He set the rake down from where he'd been gathering the leaves from his front garden. "You're late. I'm surprised. You're usually so very regimented with everything."

"*Emrys.*"

"Jonatan." He turned around, nodding to his former lover and then focusing on the young vampire at his side. They appeared to be perhaps eleven or even thirteen. It was always hard to age one of their kind. "Welcome to South Myrddin."

"This is all they have." Jonatan set two bags down. He paused before shaking his head and then turning to the child. "Emrys, meet a young Snodgrass. He'll take good care of you."

Emrys smiled gently at the young red-headed vampire. "Welcome again, foundling, to our village."

"Hello."

The word was barely audible. They'd shrunken so far into the threadbare sweater that the fabric muffled their voice. His heart ached for them.

He took a step closer to the child, crouching down to avoid looming over them. "Do you like to read?"

They finally glanced up, though their blue eyes seemed to focus on his nose, not quite meeting his gaze directly. "I love books."

"Excellent. So do I. Would you like to see my library? I made it especially for those who treasure books like the weighty gems they are. Do you have a name?" Emrys had greeted many a foundling who hadn't even been given one.

"Yes. I hate it."

"Well, then. How about I help you find one you like?" Emrys picked up their bag and led the way to his home. "Do you like tea?"

"Yes."

Emrys didn't take anything for granted. He wanted each foundling to be who they wanted to be and to choose even the simplest things. "I'll make us some tea."

They picked a book from the shelf. "I like tea and food and naps. They didn't think I made a good vampire."

"They sound like fools. Why don't you settle in for a while?" Emrys left them to peruse the shelves. He returned with tea and biscuits to find the young vampire curled up in a chair with one of his books. *"The Strange Case of Dr Jekyll and Mr Hyde.* A good read. I knew the man who loosely inspired the character. A cranky werewolf for sure, though not a monster."

"Hyde."

"Yes?"

"Hyde. I like the sound. Hyde." They repeated the name multiple times before holding out their small hand towards him. "Hyde Snodgrass."

Emrys took their hand with a smile. "A pleasure to meet you."

The End

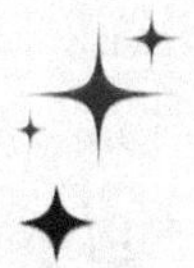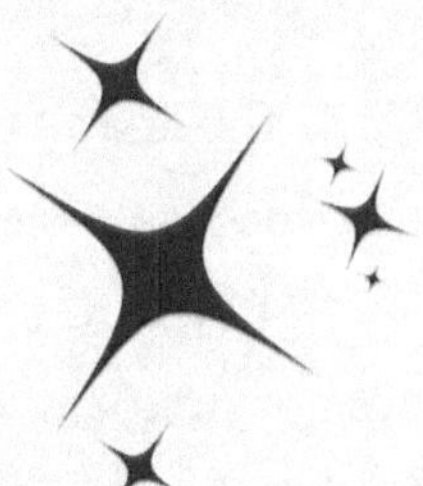

HYDE'S FIRST YULE

REUBEN

Anticipation had been building since Samhain. The turn of the wheel was taken seriously in South Myrddin; villagers made sure to celebrate to the fullest extent. Midwinter or Yule was no exception.

There were presents, lights, and decorations. Everything smelled of oranges and cloves. He had no doubts that Hyde had never experienced anything like Yule in the village.

Their little corner of South Myrddin had also been decorated. They'd come home to their temporary room at The Den to find someone had put up a Yule tree along with lights and dried oranges for decorations. It was small but festive.

"What's this?"

"Your first midwinter celebration." Reuben Ruther-

ford, the leader of the shifters in the village, stood in the doorway. He never intruded without permission.

"There are presents." Hyde pointed to the wrapped boxes next to the tree. "With my name. Presents for me."

"Village tradition. We all give each other little hand-made gifts."

"Presents." Hyde muttered the word over and over. "I haven't gotten anything for anyone."

"It's your first year." Reuben kept his distance, knowing they weren't tactile like another werewolf or shifter might be. "No one expects you to know about the traditions we have just yet."

"What do I do with them?"

Reuben was silent for a long while. He breathed out slowly, trying to release the rush of anger he had always felt at what foundlings faced. He reached out to pick one of them up. "I made this one."

"For me?"

"For you." Reuben watched the little vampire inspect all of the small presents without opening any. "We usually exchange gifts at the midwinter feast in a few days. Emrys thought you might be overwhelmed by us chucking pack-ages at you in public, so this was our next idea."

"Okay." Hyde ran their fingers over the wrapping paper again. "Not ready to open them yet."

"Take your time, wee one. They aren't going anywhere."

For the next few days, Hyde had stayed in their room. Reuben checked in on them, but they appeared to be okay. A big stack of paper had gone missing, along with scissors, glue, and a set of pencils. He had a feeling they'd decided to make something for the midwinter festival.

There was no harm in it. Reuben made sure plenty of supplies were available for their use but otherwise left them to it. Hyde, at least, remembered to come out for blood milk and snacks; they were one of the rare vampires who enjoyed eating food. He'd known plenty who preferred a liquid diet.

Quiet footsteps woke him at three in the morning on the winter solstice. He sat up in bed just in time to see an envelope shoved under his door. What in the world was the little vampire up to?

All foundlings were special. Reuben had seen many come and go in the village, though most wound up staying in South Myrddin or at least close by. There was something about Hyde that had touched all of them.

Getting out of bed, Reuben quickly dressed and quietly left his room. He followed Hyde from a distance. They walked silently through the village, slipping envelopes through letterboxes or under shop doors.

The secret mission continued until Hyde had posted all of their Yule gifts. They ended their adventure at Ada's orchard. Reuben made his presence known as they hopped up to sit on a fallen log at the edge of the property.

"The village is safe."

"Aye, it is."

"You didn't have to follow me." Hyde pouted. Their glare was as intimidating as any cub's.

"I brought you some of those cinnamon buns from the bakery." Rueben held one out to them. "They were made yesterday, but they should be just as good. You know, Santa has a reindeer; you have a werewolf."

"Emrys says Nicholas was a druid who once got very drunk, road a stag across Scotland, and left presents for people." Hyde practically inhaled the bun, shyly reaching for a second. "Emrys says the gifts he left were random twigs and things plucked from the forest on his journey."

"Emrys would know, old goat that he is. Sounds like a grand adventure. I imagine he had a very sore head in the morning." Reuben had heard variations on the legend of the midwinter gift giver. Over the years, he'd told a few of his own to the young cubs who came to stay with him. "It could be true."

"Do you think Nicholas really went around giving gifts?" Hyde finished up the last bun and began brushing a few crumbs off their cardigan.

"In my experience, folklore and myth often come from silly misadventures—usually involving druids." Reuben smiled when they glared at him again. "I'm not disparaging Emrys. But the wilder tales usually come from his kind—or the fae. In his case, it could be both."

"What about Little Red, whose grandmother ran away with a werewolf?"

"A scandalous lie. What would I want with a grandmother?" Reuben winked when Hyde shot him another glare. He heard footsteps behind them coming from the orchard. "Mornin', Ada."

"Trees whispered on the wind that I had visitors, so I brought you some warm apple and blackberry cider. A new recipe—a non-alcoholic one." Ada offered them two mugs, pulling a thermos from her pocket and pouring a portion into each one. "A blessed Yule to us all. May it be filled with joy and merriment."

Hyde clutched the mug in both hands and sighed happily. "What do you think about Little Red or Santa Claus?"

Ada leaned against one of her beloved trees. "I've never met either one personally, so I can't say for certain, though seeing isn't always believing. And I've certainly experienced enough magic in this grand world of ours to not dismiss the idea."

Hyde considered this for a second. "I'll put it on my list of folklore to research."

"A sound plan." Ada drank from her own mug of cider. "On midwinter morning, I find it easiest to believe in all manner of magic and mischief."

The End

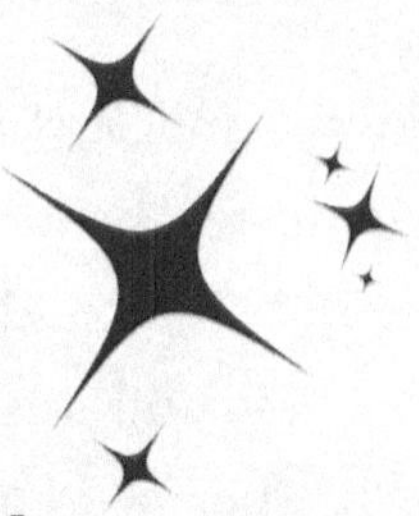

QUACK QUACK

REES

The quiet village morning was interrupted by loud quacking. Rees followed the sound down the lane from his shop and home towards Raven Park, where he found the three village crones standing in a place not far from the loch. He spotted Hyde Snodgrass in the distance.

"What's happening?" Rees joined Flossie, Winnie, and Florence in the park. They watched the little redhead chase after a duck at the edge of the loch. "Has anyone told Hyde that's a shifter and not an actual feathered friend?"

"And break their heart? Not a chance," Flossie murmured before calling out encouragement. "Be gentle, poppet. Ducks have such delicate feathers."

Rees had lived in the village for many years. Young Hyde often came by his fish and chip shop. They were

sweet and shy, totally lacking in the killer drive many vampires had. "Poor old Mallard. He won't put up with being coddled like a duckling for long."

"He will if he knows what's good for him." Winnie, with her wild purplish-grey hair and pink cardigan, smiled brightly at him. There was a definite edge to her expression. "He'll be fine."

"Did poor ole Mally do something to offend you?"

"He was less than kind to a few younger foundlings." Florence narrowed her eyes, glaring at the duck in the distance. "He can consider this his penance."

In their little village, almost everyone had arrived as a foundling. Some made their way as adults, but more often than not, they were kids or teens. Villagers tended to be protective of the youngest amongst them, understandably so. They all remembered the pain of loneliness and abandonment.

Since arriving in South Myrddin, Hyde had wormed their way into everyone's hearts. They spent a fair amount of time reading, even when they came to his chip shop. He let them hide in the back when they were having a quiet day.

He never minded. Hyde was a little mouse. They'd tried so hard not to stand out initially that it broke his heart. Time had helped them slowly blossom into themselves.

It was three days before Rees finally decided to rescue Douglas Mallard, or Mally as most called him. He'd always wondered if the duck shifter came first or the surname. It was a hilarious coincidence either way.

"Hyde?" Rees caught their attention, drawing them away from the duck, who immediately scurried off. He watched Douglas shift into his human form immediately. "Poor Mally."

"Why didn't anyone tell me that he was a shifter?" Hyde groaned when they spotted him. "It's been days. I thought he was a broken bird. Maybe no one had taught him how to… be a duck."

"C'mon, little duck. I've got a new sausage in the shop. Blatwurst. Think you're going to love it." Rees gently guided Hyde out of the park. "I'm thinking of trying a new way to cook the chips. Want to help me experiment?"

They sighed before nodding. "Fine."

Aside from bestowing Hyde with a new nickname, Rees didn't mention their attempts to teach the "duckling" how to duck. He hoped they always held that little spark of whimsy and kindness. It was a hard thing to hold on to for many in a world that tended not to treat them well.

"It'll be fun. All the chips you could possibly want." Rees patted them on the shoulder. "You're a good kid, Hyde. We're a better village with you in it."

"Yeah?" They glanced shyly up at him.

"Yeah. You know what's even better?"

"What?" Hyde asked.

"Chips."

"Chips *are* always good." Hyde was one of the rare vampires who greatly enjoyed food, even ones without blood in any shape or form. "With sausage?"

"Of course, you've worked up quite an appetite." Rees draped his arm across their shoulders. "And I got them especially with you in mind."

The End

FURRY FIENDS

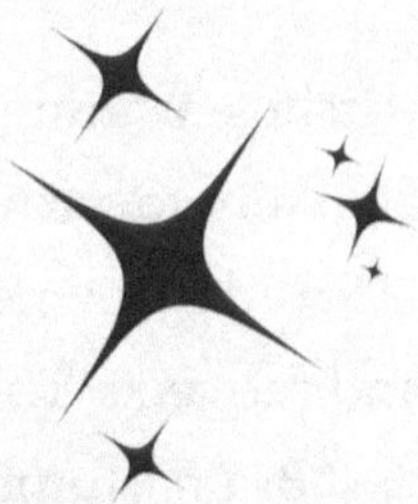

FURRY FIENDS
HYDE

The bookshop was quiet. Hyde loved the silence. But it felt empty in a way that they didn't enjoy at all.

Something was missing.

It was their first full day in their new home. Shelves were empty, for the most part. Boxes both in their apartment and in the shop were unopened. There was so much to do, yet they found themselves wandering around, doing nothing at all.

They had lived in the village for several years, staying with Emrys for a while, then having a room at The Den. But it had been time to strike out on their own. A bookshop had been the perfect solution, particularly as it had an apartment above the shop.

A knock on the door drew their attention. Hyde went over to find Flossie and Winnie, two of the local

witches, waiting for them. They both held baskets with blankets covering them.

Hyde frowned when one of the blankets squeaked and moved. "The baskets appear to be alive."

"Bram stumbled across the two little dears in the forest. All alone. Certainly not from the same litter, so I imagine they were abandoned or stolen." Winnie reached down to lift the blanket off her basket. A fluffy grey kitten sat up, meowing plaintively at Hyde. "Our wandering fae bard thought we might find a home for them."

Flossie pulled back the fabric from her basket, revealing another fluffy kitten, though this was more tabby than grey. "These two are proper familiars. They'll likely live as long as you do."

"That long?"

"There's a touch of magic to a familiar—or maybe a touch of fae." Flossie gasped when the kitten leapt out of the basket straight into Hyde's arms. "We thought about asking around the coven, but something kept suggesting that we bring them to you. We trusted our instincts; the goddess never leads us wrong."

Not to be outdone, the silvery grey kitten practically flew out of the basket at them. Hyde struggled for a second with an armful of fluff. The two scrambled up until they were sitting on Hyde's shoulders.

Frozen in place, Hyde had no idea what to do with

the two fiends perched on them. They were terrified of dislodging them and hurting them. It was clear the cats had claimed them.

What were they supposed to do with the furry beasts? Hyde had no experience with having a familiar of any sort. Vampires generally didn't, at least to their knowledge.

"I see our intuition was correct. They've chosen you," Flossie said.

Hyde blinked a few times. They glanced from one shoulder to the next, earning a gentle pat on the face for their trouble. "What do I do?"

"Florence went to gather up some supplies for you."

"But…." Hyde trailed off when the grey kitten burrowed into the collar of their cardigan. "Cats?"

"They are good guardians and friends." Flossie took both of the blankets from the baskets and handed them to Hyde. "They love being cosy."

"As do I." Hyde clutched the blankets tightly while trying not to dislodge the kittens. "Do they have names?"

"Not yet. We haven't had much time with them since Bram brought them to us. Mostly, they slept or seemed utterly enraptured by the mortar and pestle in my kitchen." Winnie chuckled when the orange fluff-ball tucked their head against Hyde's neck. "They've certainly chosen you."

"Mortar and Pestle." Hyde glanced to their left and right. The kittens purred almost in unison, rubbing against either side of their neck. "Welcome home?"

Flossie reached out to gently pat Hyde on the shoulder, deftly avoiding the swiping cat paw. "Yes, I do believe you've found the perfect companions."

"We'll be by later with supplies," Winnie told them.

Hyde stared dumbfounded as the two witches sauntered off, murmuring to each other while swinging the baskets merrily at their sides. They watched until one of the kittens bopped their wee head against their cheek. "Right. Mortar and Pestle. Is purring good? Purring is definitely good. It has to be."

Returning to the bookshop, Hyde expected them to jump off their shoulders, but the kittens seemed quite content to perch up there like a pair of parrots. They stayed there while Hyde made a slow circuit around the room.

They showed their new familiars around the mostly empty space. There were glimpses of what the shop might become, from the rug that one of the villagers had brought over to their favourite comfy chair from Emrys's library that he'd gifted and the faerie lights strung along the top of all the shelves. The three inspected the upstairs apartment before returning downstairs.

"That's the fireplace. Emrys worked his magic with Morrigan. It won't do any harm to the books." Hyde ran their fingers along the mantle. "It's empty, but not for long. We'll make it home."

The meow and chirp from either side of them seemed like agreement. Hyde sat in their chair in front of the fireplace. The kittens curled up on the blanket stretched across their lap.

"I hope you like books and naps. We're going to have loads of both." Hyde adjusted the blankets to make sure they were comfortable.

The shop had seemed so empty earlier. Now, all Hyde felt was the fire's warmth and the kittens' gentle purring. It was somehow less intimidating than it had been.

"I can do this." Hyde glanced down at two very insistent squeaky meows. "*We* can do this. It's going to be brilliant."

The End

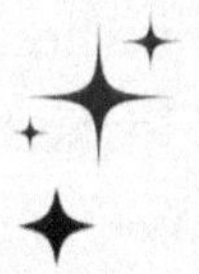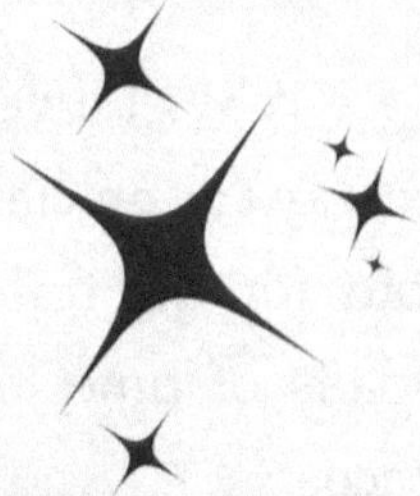

LOVE AT FIRST BITE
HYDE

"It's a taco truck."

"Bus. Technically, it's a bus." Hyde stared at the vehicle being parked adjacent to the bookshop. "A vintage double-decker bus."

"It has an apartment upstairs and a fully functional but small restaurant-grade kitchen." Emrys stood beside them as they watched the bus slowly reversing into position. "Are you sure you don't mind?"

"I'm going to have tacos in front of my shop. Tacos. I can get them anytime I want." Hyde had never been more excited for a new addition to the village. "And Teresa promised to look into making ones with blood sausage. There's apparently a recipe in her family grimoire."

"I was worried."

"Why? I love tacos." Hyde leaned into Emrys. They always appreciated how much he cared for and looked out for the foundlings in the village. "You gave me loads of time to consider it. And I like Teresa. I like tacos."

"Do you?"

"Why does everyone sound odd when I say I like Teresa?" Hyde had heard Flossie, Winnie, Florence, and others, all with the same lilt in their voices. "She's a nice witch. Mortar and Pestle approve of her."

"Always good to have feline approval."

"She's nice. She liked my signs." Hyde nodded back towards the bookshop, where Hello and They were visible on the counter. "She already placed an order for a few graphic novels. It will be brilliant to have tacos outside my front door. Not literally. I'll have to walk to get them."

"I…." Emrys gave them a look they didn't understand. It was almost as if he knew something, but they had no idea what. "I'm sure it will be incredibly nice."

Hyde lifted the bag in their hands. "I got her a 'welcome to this corner of the village' gift. It's a tiny avocado plushie."

"I'm sure she'll love it."

"I'm going to give it to her." Hyde hadn't moved so much as a muscle yet. They paused. "I am."

"I promise she'll love it." Emrys placed a comforting hand on their shoulder. "Go on, foundling."

After another moment of hesitation, Hyde turned away from him. They crossed the short distance to the taco truck. Teresa glanced up expectantly from where she'd been testing the serving windows, which had been custom-fitted to the side of the double-decker bus.

"A present." Hyde shoved the bag into Teresa's hands. "It's for you. Okay. Bye."

Fleeing back to the safety of the bookshop, Hyde leaned against the closed door. Mortar and Pestle immediately rushed over, or as hurried as their feline friends ever were. The two rubbed against their legs, offering support.

Hyde jumped when someone knocked on the door. They'd been standing there far longer than they thought. *I am being ridiculous.*

Taking a second to collect themselves, Hyde finally twisted around and opened the door. Teresa smiled brightly. They almost slammed it shut again, feeling an odd sense of embarrassment or some emotion they couldn't identify rush through them.

"Hello." Hyde had never been brilliant with new people. It usually took them a while to warm up to them. "Hi."

"I had some ingredients already prepped so I could experiment and perhaps offer samples. I'm not ready to open up the shop quite yet." Teresa smiled brightly. "I brought you the first tacos."

Hyde reached out hesitantly for the plate. "Smells divine."

"Family recipe."

"Sometimes those are the best kind." Hyde had mixed feelings about the concept of family, but not when it came to tacos. "Thank you."

"There are a few treats for your cats as well." Teresa gave that bright smile again, which made a weird little flutter happen in Hyde's stomach. "Hope you enjoy. Thank you for the avocado. I adore it."

"We will. Have to go now." Hyde retreated into the store and shut the door—slowly to avoid seeming desperate or rude. They once again leaned against it and closed their eyes. A quiet cough from across the room caught their attention. "I can hear you silently mocking me."

"I would never. That was brave of you."

"Was it?" Hyde opened one eye to find Emrys walking towards them. "It felt silly."

"It was." Emrys went over to the shop counter, setting Mortar on it. "Now, stop holding the door upright and help me find a new book to read."

"You have an entire library."

"There are never enough books to read, Hyde. Never." Emrys made an excellent point. "What new finds have you brought to us?"

The End

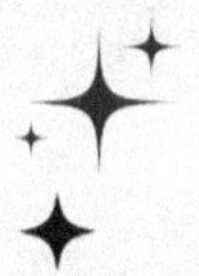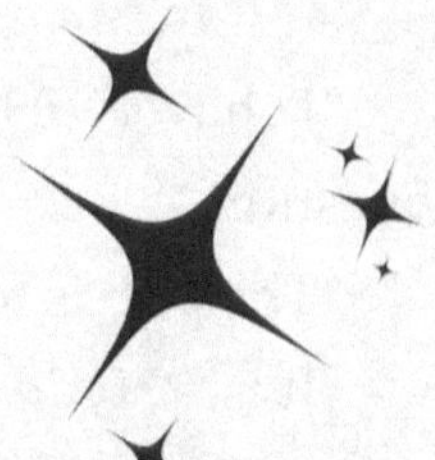

THE SKELETON CREW

HYDE

When Florence came into the bookshop, Hyde was immediately suspicious. Not of the witch's presence, but of the way she'd moved around the shop. She appeared to be looking around as if she'd never been into Between the Leaves, which she had a hundred times or more.

"You have this lovely open space by the hearth."

"I believe I sense a conspiracy." Hyde clutched Pestle in their arms, murmuring against his fluffy ginger head. "It's distinctly crone-like with a hint of witch."

"Don't be rude, poppet." Florence lifted the large quilted bag she'd brought with her. "You've been enjoying knitting with us at the pub; I thought you'd like this to keep your projects in."

"I have." Hyde knew it sounded more like a question.

"The pub is too rowdy for a knitting club."

"It is." Hyde cuddled Pestle more tightly, letting his engine-like purring keep them calm. "The bookshop isn't."

"No, it isn't. We could meet once a week—a very small group of yarn enthusiasts. Tea and snacks would, of course, be a necessity." Florence smiled when Hyde perked up at that. "We could be silent on the days you need us to be. And you'd have the final say on who would be welcome."

"Might be fun." Hyde picked up the scrimshaw knitting needles that had been gifted to them. "I don't have enough chairs."

"Why don't we bring our own—if you approve of them?"

Hyde closed their eyes briefly, trying to imagine the space. "It might be cosy to have loads of different armchairs. People could read in them when we weren't knitting."

"Plenty of places for your furry familiars to sleep." Florence tapped a finger gently against Pestle's head. "Have a think on it for a few days before you decide. It's always wise to give yourself time to process first."

"Okay."

For a week, Hyde had considered the idea. The first few days, they hadn't thought about it at all. And then, it had been all they could think about.

Standing in the bookshop, Hyde surveyed the open space near the fireplace. They shifted the small table off to the side, then pulled back the little couch and the solitary armchair. It allowed plenty of room for others.

It was cosy by the fire. Hyde could imagine a little group knitting or crocheting, sharing snacks and tea or wine. They thought it might be good.

"Knock, knock." Teresa stepped into the bookshop. Her gaze darted to the Hello sign on the counter before taking in the changes. "Rearranging the furniture?"

"We're going to start a knitting club. Do you knit?" Hyde was suddenly even more excited about the prospect. Perhaps it would give them a way to become even closer to Teresa. "Or crochet?"

"I can learn."

They stood in the now-cleared space in silence for a moment. Hyde picked up their project bag and showed Teresa their latest cardigan. She seemed especially interested in the carved bone knitting needles.

"Does it have a name? Your club?"

"Not yet." Hyde put the cardigan away. "It needs one."

Teresa leaned in to further inspect the delicately carved tools that had been a gift. "How about the Skeleton Crew?"

"After the needles?" Hyde lifted one up to look at the tiny skull at the top. "The Skeleton Crew. I like it."

"So, why clear out so much space?" Teresa crouched down to greet Pestle and Mortar, who'd deigned to leave their comfortable spots by the fireplace.

"Everyone is going to bring their favourite chairs." Hyde continued to warm to the idea the more they considered it. "A hodgepodge of furniture. I think I'd prefer that to a matched set. It's more cosy."

"More you—more Between the Leaves."

"It will be fun." Hyde's gaze darted to Teresa, then back to the cats. "An evening with the fireplace going, music playing, food to eat, and crafting."

"It will definitely be fun." Teresa sat on the floor with the cats, laughing when they immediately collapsed in her lap. "Maybe you can teach me how to knit?"

"I… I could do that." Hyde turned around and began putting away their cardigan project. Their fingers trembled while gently slipping it back into the bag. "I think."

"You'll be a brilliant teacher." Teresa spoke so confidently that Hyde almost believed her. "Do you have any preferred snacks? The first official meeting of our club should have good ones."

"Anything you make." Hyde cringed at how quickly the words flew out. That had definitely been too honest. If vampires blushed, they were definitely doing it. "Tacos… are good."

"They are." Teresa gave them a bright smile before returning her attention to the cats in her lap. "I'm glad I moved here."

"So am I."

The End

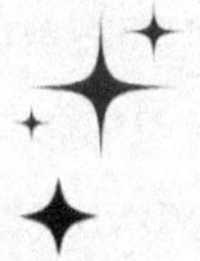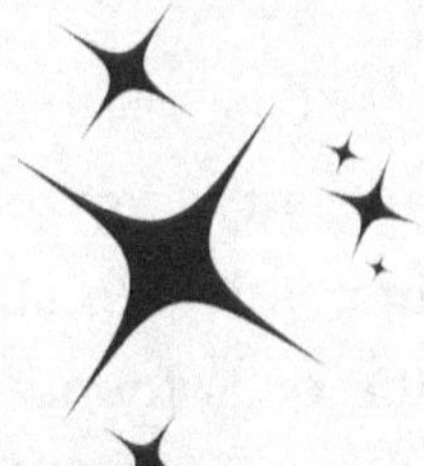

THE LEGEND OF KING ARTHUR

HYDE

Hyde climbed the winding stairs leading up to the top of the lighthouse. They finally reached the landing, finding Bram sitting on a pile of cushions with his guitar in hand. "Morrigan said you knew about King Arthur."

Bram gently laid his guitar to one side. He pulled out a delicately carved pipe, added a mixture of herbs, and then snapped his fingers, lighting it. A sweet, floral scent soon filled the air around them. "King? Make yourself comfortable. I'll tell you about Arthur, the supposed Welsh ruler who somehow made it to the Highlands."

"Supposed?"

"He wasn't Arthur or a king. Far more fable to his story than truth." Bram stretched his long legs out. "Why the sudden interest?"

"One of the book hunters I work with found an ancient copy of the *Historia Brittonum*. It's almost impossible to authenticate. Experts still argue whether the ones found after the eleventh century were forgeries or not." Hyde continued to ramble about the *History of Britons*, believed to be from around the eighth or ninth century, for a moment. They gave a sheepish smile after a while. "Sorry. The history and provenance of books are fascinating."

"They are." Bram nudged their knee with his foot. "So? Arthur?"

"There's mention of him there. A few times." Hyde hadn't been able to stop themselves from talking to Morrigan about it while at the post office. "Did you know him?"

"Are you trying to say I'm old enough to know a supposed king from the eighth century?" Bram glowered at them before grinning to show he'd been joking. "A fair shot. I am fae."

"That's not an answer," Hyde huffed.

"I knew an Arthur. Or Artair as he was known then. One of my many jaunts out of the fae realm." Bram puffed on his pipe for a moment. "I could sing you a tale."

"Or just tell me?"

"Careful, *mo chridhe*. You might hurt my feelings. I'm a delicate flower." Bram chuckled when Hyde tossed a pebble at him. "All right, all right. They got the century correct. Not the location. It wasn't Wales; it was here. Not South Myrddin specifically, but the general area."

"Here? But the *Historia Brittonum*...."

"Ah. But I'm telling this story. You'd have loved it, Hyde. The ancient world, in general, but the Highlands have always been magical." Bram described Scotland of old in such detail that they felt they were there. "I grant you there were downsides to it. Illnesses with no cure. No indoor plumbing. Constant wars."

"Not to mention the fate of foundlings like me?"

"Best not think on that too much." Bram frowned. He seemed lost in thought for a moment before forcing a smile back on his face.

In no time at all, Hyde was carried away by images of ancient castles and battles. He described a Highlands that they had never known. It reminded them of tapestries they'd once seen while visiting one of the few intact fortresses still remaining.

"Arthur, like most wealthy and powerful men, thought himself a grand leader. A king. The head of the largest pack of werewolves at the time. They ran wild through the Highlands." Bram puffed on his pipe again, sending cheerful clouds of smoke floating past. "They were obnoxious."

"So, what happened?"

"Heavy is the head…."

"Bram."

"Those who build wooden palaces should not light bonfires indoors. Metaphorically speaking." Bram was, as always, amused at their annoyance. "He angered far too many with his dreams."

"That is *not* an answer."

He heaved a dramatic sigh. "They tried to control the Highlands. Arthur wanted to truly be king."

"Wasn't there already one?"

"Several, plus chieftains. But Arthur, he of the over-sized ego, thought he could rule the world or at least a portion of it. Ended badly. He wasn't as charming, rich, powerful, or connected as others." Bram described the final, ugly battle that had ended with a massive fire. It had destroyed everything in its path, leaving nothing behind. "No one was really left from his side of the fight. There was little mercy in those days."

"So, no Camelot, no round table?" Hyde felt a little let down, though it wasn't the first time they'd found more fiction than fact when it came to ancient history.

"Camelot? Only in dreams and imaginations." Bram chuckled when they scowled at him. "I suppose I helped the legend take flight."

"Did you? Why am I not surprised?"

"I may have sung a few songs long after the pack had died out. Laid the foundation for King Arthur and his knights." He was entirely unrepentant, as he always was when making mischief. "I threw a rock in the pond; I never imagined the ripples would carry so far and wide."

Hyde narrowed their eyes, trying to assess the truth of his words. It was always hard to tell with Bram. "That does sound like something you would do."

"What can I say? I am the creator of legend."

The End

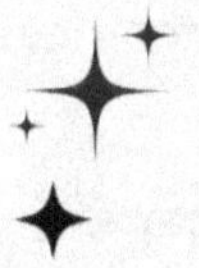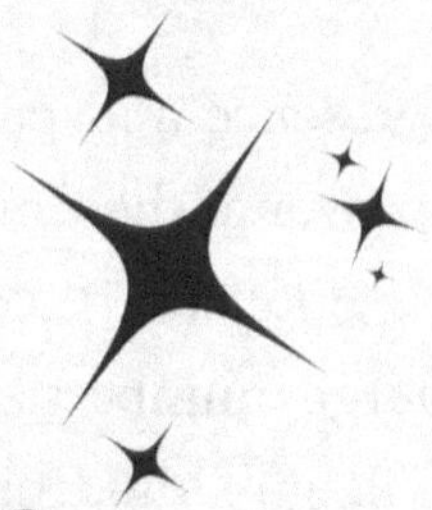

FAE IN THE FOG
BRAM

Arguments could be made about who arrived in the Highlands first. Bram knew the fae had stepped on plush green hills far earlier than most. They had simply never left a tangible trace, not in ways historians could or would follow.

There were few written histories of the fae. No coven grimoires to hold their secrets. Fewer works of folklore that actually got it right. Their stories had been passed down from the oldest of them to the youngest.

It was short-sighted, in his opinion. One might tell a story one way, while another had a different version. He supposed it added to the mystery surrounding the fae; perhaps that was the true purpose.

The fae had purposefully withdrawn from this realm, leaving a fog of confusion surrounding their

presence and past. They had vast amounts of magical power at their fingertips. Isolation suited them.

Outside of court meetings, they rarely gathered in large numbers. He had been an outlier. Life in the village suited him for a time, though the siren call of wandering tugged at his feet.

Bram was certainly not the eldest fae in existence, though perhaps in Scotland. He did have memories of early visits from the realm. His brand of chaos had never been fully accepted by his own. It had seemed fortuitous when South Myrddin was founded.

A place for the abandoned.

A place for the odd ones.

A place for those searching for home.

The foundlings had come to mean a great deal to him. He had been welcomed by them. Something that hadn't always happened in the Unseelie Court.

Bram found his feet guiding him through the village to Between the Leaves. He opened the door and stepped into Hyde's bookshop. "Morning."

"You'll never guess what I've found." Hyde held up a tiny leather-bound tome. "*Fae in the Fog.*"

Bram schooled his features to avoid laughing outright. He didn't want them to misunderstand his amusement. "Ah. Yes. It's absolute nonsense."

"What? How do you know?" Hyde came around the counter, flipping through the book. "Everything I could find says it's the only true written history of the fae."

"All horseshite."

"And you know this how?"

"I wrote it."

"*Bram.*" Hyde swatted him on the arm. "Why?"

"My sincerest apologies, *mo chairde.*" He knew they considered books to be almost sacred things. "A… mistake I made in my youth."

"What, at the dawn of time?" Emrys spoke from where he'd been hiding in the far corner of the shop, seated in a large armchair with a book in hand. "I did warn you, foundling, that it might not be a legitimate find."

"In fairness, it is an original edition of a very old book. It also happens to be mostly fiction with very little fact." Bram felt a sliver of guilt go through him at Hyde's disappointed sigh.

They grumbled under their breath in what he thought might be Gaelic, but it was too quiet for him to hear. "I was so excited about finally finding even a little of the fae's history in written form."

"I am sorry."

Hyde glowered. It was a little like being glared at by a kitten. "Books aren't your playthings. You shouldn't claim fiction as fact. There lies danger."

Bram raised his hands and apologised once again

when the cats hissed at him. He knew he had to make amends. "Forgive me?"

"Probably."

Bram stretched his long legs out in front of him, getting more comfortable in his chosen armchair. "Truth be told, *mo chairde*, none of us know fact from fiction for certain. With no written history, we have our family stories. I can only share what they believed to be true. And I have told you about being cautious when it comes to the fae."

Gathering his thoughts, Bram considered which story to tell. He accepted a mug of tea from Hyde. They went to sit near the fireplace, getting comfortable while Emrys occasionally looked up from his book to glower at him.

To his great amusement and mild irritation, Emrys had clearly decided to remain. They'd never been the closest of friends. Bram knew he'd gone out of his way to aggravate the old druid whenever possible; he couldn't help himself.

If nothing else, Bram hoped Emrys trusted him never to hurt one of the foundlings, especially Hyde. He'd grown incredibly fond of the vampire. They both shared a love of the written word and of stories.

Bram selected his favourite of the armchairs. He took a drink of the tea, which was made perfectly for him. Hyde had a knack for getting it made the way he preferred, not that he'd ever have complained otherwise.

"Story time." Hyde had gathered their two cats into their lap, somehow managing them and a mug of blood-laced tea without upending it. All three stared at him expectantly. "Right?"

"Right."

"Fact, not fiction." Hyde clearly felt the need to reiterate.

"As best as I can tell."

Sinking into his memories, Bram told the tale his grandfather had shared with him. The one about the first fae who journeyed out of the realm into the world. Those who decided to explore what might exist outside the court.

His grandfather had been one to speak through stories. Bram thought he would've adored Hyde. Kindred spirits who appreciated truthful tales as much as tall ones.

For many centuries, there were some who claimed the fae were the first beings to exist. Bram disagreed vehemently. It was delusions of grandeur that made them think such.

"My grandfather used to say we were formed from lost souls who made their way into the otherworld where nought but magic resides. Wee bairns who died too young and couldn't find their way to the ferryman." Bram had always thought it as sweet an explanation as any he'd heard. "Given how long the fae have existed and the near-immortal length of our lives, I have my doubts."

"That's a tall tale."

"One of his favourites."

Smiling at the belaboured sigh from his vampire friend, Bram moved on to stories with more of a ring of truth. He spoke of how an ancient druid wielded magic near one of the strongest ley lines in the Highlands, opening up a gateway by pure accident. From the description, he'd always had a suspicion it had been Myrddin himself.

To his knowledge, it was not the fae's first visit to the mortal world. The gateway still stood, hidden in a protected glade near what had once been Castle MacDougal. Loch Ness was and would always be a powerful, sacred site to all, especially the fae.

"My grandfather always claimed we took our form from humans. I've never seen another fae appear different. No wings. Or different ears like in fairy tales." Bram had his own theories, but they would only muddy the water. "There are also those who believe we were the beginnings of life here."

"Proven wrong by both history and science."

"Correct."

"Maybe the tall tales are more interesting." Hyde

was staring mulishly into the fireplace. "What about those? Sometimes, there's a sliver of truth in the fables and folklore."

"You're not wrong. It's far easier to tell you what isn't true than what is." Bram had a collection of stories somewhere amongst his belongings. He wondered if he could dig the book out for Hyde. He trusted them to not share it around. "*Fae in the Fog* might be fiction, but they were things I'd heard spoken as truth."

Picking up the book, Bram skimmed through the various fanciful fae origin stories. He spoke about the myth of a great goddess who blew on a dandelion, spreading seeds across the worlds—and creating the Seelie and Unseelie Courts in the process.

"A dandelion and a goddess?" Hyde muttered the question, scratching the ear of one of the cats. "Sounds remarkably like one of the stories from Shikobi's Choctaw elders."

"You'll find, as you study the histories of many magical cultures, there's a thread of similarity amongst them." Emrys set aside his book to join the conversation. "Part of what binds us together, if we'll let it."

The End

ACKNOWLEDGMENTS

A massive thank-you to my brilliant betas and the crew in my Cozies by the Fire group who helped brainstorm some of the names in the book. To Becky, Kristin, and all the fantastic people at Tangled Tree and Hot Tree Publishing. And also to my beloved hubby, who I lost in March 2025. He always supported my writing, and I miss him every single day.

And, finally, thank you, readers, for following me on my writing journey.

ABOUT THE AUTHOR

Dahlia Donovan wrote her first romance series after a crazy dream about shifters and damsels in distress. She prefers irreverent humour and unconventional characters. An autistic and occasional hermit, she has found great happiness with her husband, her tiny dog Bacon, and her collection of books and video games.

Don't miss out on new releases, exclusive giveaways, and much more!

Join Dahlia's newsletter:

http://eepurl.com/Q0n0X

Join her reader group:

www.facebook.com/groups/1108750876162947

She'd love to hear from you directly, too. Please feel free to email her at dahlia@dahliadonovan.com or check out her website https://dahliadonovan.com/ for updates.

facebook.com/dahliadonovan

instagram.com/dahliadonovanauthor

pinterest.com/dahliadonovan

ABOUT THE PUBLISHER

Hot Tree Publishing loves love. Publishing adult romantic fiction, HTPubs are all about diverse reads featuring heroes and heroines to swoon over. Since opening in 2015, HTPubs have published more than 300 titles across the wide and diverse range of romantic genres. If you're chasing a happily ever after in your favourite subgenre, HTPubs have you covered.

Interested in discovering more amazing reads brought to you by Hot Tree Publishing? Head over to the website for information:

WWW.HOTTREEPUBLISHING.COM

facebook.com/hottreepublishing

instagram.com/hottreepublishing

tiktok.com/@hottreepublishing

www.ingramcontent.com/pod-product-compliance
Lightning Source LLC
Chambersburg PA
CBHW050608190726
48283CB00007B/2324